AND SO
TO
SLEEP

EVELYN ALLEN HARPER

ISBN 978-1-60910-622-5

BookLocker.com, Inc.
2010

Second Edition

To my two sisters,
Ruby and Norma,
who wouldn't let me quit.

ACKNOWLEDGEMENT

WHEN AN ACCIDENT OCCURS, you can blame it on someone or you can accept the blame and admit it was your fault. The accident in question is my writing the Accidental Mystery Series.

The first to blame would be my two sisters who hounded me for 'and then what happened?' e-mails. I wrote freely and copiously, knowing no matter what silliness I came up with, they would love it. The stories were for their eyes. Their only request was that I wouldn't write anything that would embarrass them.

And then on Tuesdays nights I sing with a group of Sweet Adelines, an international organization of women who sing four-part a cappella harmony. Being surrounded by rich chords gives me such a high, sleep is elusive on those nights and I can easily knock off several chapters. I can blame them for the volume of the books. When I needed to explain Molly's 'magic' pills, pharmacist Tracy Haver, a bass in that organization, put it in terms that even I could understand. Polly Penwell, a friend who both sings and writes with me, helped me put the story in terms that hopefully you, the reader, can understand.

There is a writing group that I stumbled onto after I had written the first book and half of the second book. I can blame them for liking what I wrote and encouraged me to continue, even though they were surprised at how much I didn't know about writing techniques. They were patient teachers.

Roberta Jean Bryant (see blurb), you had a hand in this, too. Not only did you read my book, you had the audacity to make constructive suggestions. The name, Accidental Mystery Series, was your brainchild. Don't try to deny it; I saved the e-mail.

Readers, I hope you stick with me throughout the entire three book series: And So To Sleep, And So To Dream, and The Wrath of Grapes.

INTRODUCTION

AS I WRITE THIS, it is 4:53 A.M. I have not slept despite taking my prescribed medication. My legs feel like they are being electrocuted.

I have had the misfortune of having crazy legs most of my life. I lived in an area where doctors offered nothing but sympathy and speeches about stress and depression.

In 1996, I moved to northern Michigan where my condition was correctly diagnosed and my crazy leg problem finally had a name; Restless Leg Syndrome.

There are medications now for RLS; sometime they work, and sometimes they don't.

The following story was written during the nights when the medication was not working.

PROLOGUE

FOR WANT OF ANOTHER NAME, she called him the leg demon. He usually visited her earlier in the evening, but tonight he waited until she was sound asleep before he announced his presence. She tried to ignore the buzz he was causing in her legs, but he won. He always won.

The buzz sensation quickly built in intensity until, at the very peak, her legs kicked in protest.

Before the next build-up and kick, she jumped out of bed.

CHAPTER 1

"DAMN LEGS!" Molly muttered as she pulled the door closed behind her. Shivering, she paused to button her jacket. The midnight darkness morphed the neighborhood houses into unfamiliar shapes and, for a brief moment, a sense of uneasiness made her wonder if this was such a good idea. Dismissing her apprehension with a shrug, she began to walk. With a feeling of envy, she pictured the people in the dark houses all snug in bed asleep the way she longed to be.

Tonight, it was the buzzing demon that had kicked her out of bed, but she was well acquainted with others. The burning, creepy-crawly, tingling, pulling ones visited her regularly. Moving her legs was the only relief; she put her head down and grimly started, one foot in front of the other.

Damn legs!

Dogs, aware of a walker, responded. From house to house, a steady chorus of barks traced her progress. Imagining how irritated the residents were at their barking pets gave her a perverse sense of satisfaction. If she couldn't sleep, why should they?

A spot of interest in her otherwise boring walk was an alley that ran behind a row of houses. The only property owner living in the short alley that connected two main streets was the McGuire family. Over time, the alley took on the name of that family and the residents of the area referred to it as McGuire's Alley. Mr. McGuire collected junk. Why the city council allowed such a pile of trash in the middle of town was a mystery until

Molly did some research; Mr. McGuire was a member of that council.

The neighborhood boys, using the streetlights for target practice, had added darkness to the decrepit atmosphere of the alley. In summer when the days were long and it would still be light when she started her walk, she often included a hike down the alley just to break the routine.

One working street light assured her that nothing had changed. There was a large collection of rubbish, but it was the tidily arranged front line that amused her.

Mr. McGuire, or maybe it was Mrs. McGuire, must have some civic pride, or maybe a case of Obsessive Compulsive Disorder, if you considered how nicely the trash was arranged according to height. The tallest item, a refrigerator with the door missing, was first in line. Following that was a car with most of its parts gone. A large sofa and its matching love seat ended the collection. All items were far past being usable.

She was about to resume her walk when she heard men's voices and saw movement around the junked refrigerator. She peered down the alley chuckling to herself that someone might actually be stealing McGuire's junk. Disappointed when nothing happened, she resumed her walk.

Damn legs.

She sighed with relief when the walk brought her back to her own house. Sitting on the porch step to catch her breath, she looked at the quiet street. Even though she didn't know her neighbors by name, she had met some of them at a block party. She grinned, remembering the frantic chase through numerous backyards trying to catch a lost dog. After that, whenever she drove by, her neighbors waved and smiled at her.

She had done her homework before buying the house; nothing much ever happened in this part of town. At least it hadn't until

AND SO TO SLEEP

lately. The smashed streetlights made her wonder if things were changing in the neighborhood.

Before she had a chance to enjoy the soft night air, the demon was back.

While she was walking a bit slower the second time around the block, the sound of activity again coming from the junk area made her feel uneasy. She stopped. Up until now, imagining that something was happening in McGuire's Alley was just a ploy to make her tedious walk a bit more interesting. She stood by the entrance to the alley, curious, but not curious enough to investigate. When a muffled shout raised the hair on her arms, she headed for home. Maybe she had walked enough tonight.

AT FOUR O'CLOCK in the morning, a visiting demon sent electric shocks through her left leg. Jumping out of bed and grabbing her robe, Molly sighed as she headed for the den. She was sure this was how it would feel if her leg were actually plugged into a light socket.

Damn legs!

CHAPTER 2

THE ONE WORKING streetlight in McGuire's Alley threw the shadow of a tall, skinny man hovering over two unmoving lumps on the ground. Sammy the Grunt, his long gray hair streaming over his face, wiped the blood off his knife and grinned. Using his foot, he rolled one of the lumps over and spit. No one, not even old friends from Chicago, robbed Sammy and got away with it. Sammy and his sidekicks, Clarence and Albert, had interrupted two thieves stealing their stashed drugs in the junked refrigerator.

It was only after he had killed the two thieves that Sammy looked around and found that he was alone. The rage building inside him was at the boiling point when he saw Albert and Clarence running toward him from the alley's entrance.

"Where the hell have you been?" he whispered through clenched teeth.

"We was your lookouts!" panted Clarence.

Sammy was ready for them, knife flashing, and murder in his eyes. Albert pushed away the arm holding the knife and said quietly, "We have a problem."

"No, *you* have a problem!" Sammy declared, poking Albert's chest with the knife.

"We seen a woman walker!" blurted Clarence. It scared him when Sammy got like this.

Startled, Sammy hissed, "A witness? Hell, she could send us away for eternity! I want that woman found, and I want her *permanently* silenced. Understand?"

14

Seeing the perplexed expression on Clarence's face, he added, "Albert, make sure your little buddy knows what that big word means."

Clarence hung his head.

"Now, back to you two," Sammy said as the bloody knife reappeared. "If you pull a disappearin' act on me again...," he threatened, waving the knife.

Clarence and Albert stepped back.

"Put that knife away," Albert grumbled. "Haven't you done enough damage already?"

Sammy whirled, pointed the knife at Albert, and then lowered it. "Anything else I should know about?"

"I seen a firefly," Clarence announced.

"Mama's little boy saw a firefly?" sneered Sammy. "Grow up!"

Watching Sammy's reaction to this bit of news, Clarence decided this was not a good time to tell him he had seen not one but two fireflies. The ones he had remembered seeing as a young boy hadn't made a clicking sound when they lit up like these two had, but the flash was just the same.

"Where do we go now, Sammy?" Clarence shuddered. "I don't like being here with those dead guys."

"We're goin' back to the McGuire house."

"Sammy," Albert questioned, "do you really think it's safe to use McGuire's house now?"

"Everyone in town knows the family is off on vacation and as long as we don't turn on lights, I doubt the police will give McGuire's house a second thought," Sammy said, and he and Clarence stepped off into the black night.

Albert watched Clarence and Sammy the Grunt disappear into the darkness. Bile rose in his throat and he swallowed hard. He muttered a few words over the bodies and headed for the McGuire house.

A SECURITY GUARD driving home from his night shift at the airport took a shortcut through McGuire's Alley. His call to 911 brought bright lights and a swarm of law enforcers to the quiet neighborhood. Curiosity seekers poured out of their houses in pajamas and robes, horrified at the violence that had taken place on their quiet street.

One of the officials, Detective Mitch Hatch, was interviewing a man who nervously clutched his beltless robe. He assured the detective that he had been in bed since the eleven o'clock news and had nothing to tell. As he was about to walk away, he called back over his shoulder, "Maybe you should ask that lady."

"What lady?" asked Detective Hatch.

"The one who walks most nights, that's who!"

"What's her name?"

"I don't know," said the man as he kept walking, "but I know where she lives."

"Can you point out her house?"

The man stopped, looked down at his robe, shrugged, and then said, "Follow me."

Detective Hatch followed the man to the end of the alley and looked at the house where the man was pointing. "I've seen her go into that house lots of times."

"Did you ever speak to her?"

"Never did. But I know she leaves every morning around eight o'clock."

"Do you have any idea where the lady works?"

"No," the man replied, "but one day I saw her put signs in the trunk of her car."

"What kind of signs?"

"Some kind of real estate signs. Now can I go home?"

Detective Hatch shook the man's hand, thanked him, and went back to the crime scene. First thing tomorrow, he would go into his office computer, and, with the address of the woman's house, find the name of the owner.

Chapter 3

THE ALARM WENT off by Molly's bedside at six thirty. Without opening her eyes, she reached out her arm to stop the jarring racket. A new day was beginning, and she had the feeling this day was going to be a repeat of many other days.

By day, Molly Allen was a successful Realtor. Her dad had started Allen Real Estate before she had graduated from Michigan State.

Molly loved the northern Michigan area. She never tired of visiting the small towns that nestled in the middle of sand dunes and glacial potholes. The potholes with natural springs became the ring of small lakes that dotted the landscape.

It was in one of these small towns that her dad had chosen to open his office. Later, when he became ill, Molly gladly left her teaching position, got her real estate license and went to work for him. After his death, she took over the business.

By night, she was, well, she didn't know what she was.

When, as a child, she had described the peculiar feelings in her legs, the pediatrician assured her parents that it was nothing more than growing pains. As she matured, the problem became worse and the need to move her legs became stronger. Most nights, the urge was strong enough to drive her out of bed. In bad weather, she walked inside; in good weather, she walked through her neighborhood.

The sensations in her legs were hard to explain. The last time she tried, her doctor had listened to her patiently, then patted her on the back and handed her a prescription; it was a referral to a psychiatrist. She'd learned her lesson well. Since moving here and taking over her dad's business, she'd never mentioned her strange problem to the local doctors.

Pulling the covers over her head, she thought about last night. Walking twice around the block had chased away the demon, but not permanently. When he visited her again at four o'clock in the morning, she headed for the den where she'd left her library book on the coffee table. It was a good mystery, and it held her interest even though she read it while she walked. Occasionally she leaned against the wall, feeling exhausted, but she knew better than to sit down. Her legs would only allow her to sit for a minute or two and then they would demand that she move them again. Reading until her eyes burned, she put the book down and made her way to bed where she fell into a deep sleep until the unwelcome sound of the alarm woke her.

Reluctantly crawling out of bed, she had to admit that she felt much older than her thirty-five years. A glance in the mirror on her way to the shower confirmed it.

As she dressed for work, her mind focused on the coming day. She had made appointments to show houses to a family this morning.

The new buyers were a referral from a satisfied customer. After fifteen years in real estate, most of her business came from successful past transactions. She joked with her widowed mother that she didn't have to advertise her services anymore because most of her business now was like picking low-hanging fruit. Her mother had smiled and held her tongue. This was when she usually pointed out that Molly wouldn't have to work so hard if she had a husband. Molly appreciated that her mother hadn't pursued the subject because it never went anywhere or helped anything.

Thinking about her mother always gave her concern. Widowed quite young, Peggy Allen had chosen to stay in the large family house. Tom, Molly's brother, had moved out after he graduated from college, and Molly had tried to talk her mother into buying a condominium. Molly shook these thoughts from her head. She had a day of showing houses to think about.

A two-piece red dress in the back of her closet caught her eye. The color red always made her feel strong, and today, after an almost sleepless night, she needed help anywhere she could get it.

Studying the mirror's reflection of her newly dried hair, she considered her choices: up or down. Deciding that she wanted to make a serious impression, she gathered her long red hair, pulled it off her face, and pinned it to the top of her head.

She liked to think the effect made her look taller than her height of five feet and one half inch; standing slightly on her toes when her height was measured accounted for the half inch. Because there would be a lot of walking today, she slipped her feet into comfortable shoes. The last thing she did was to look at her face in the mirror. The dark circles under her puffy tired eyes looked a little less dark after she applied makeup. A bit of pink on the cheeks and a smear of pink lip-gloss finished the job.

Stepping back from the mirror, she inspected her reflected image. What she saw was a pretty face with a dimple in each cheek, an unremarkable nose, and green eyes that might just be her best feature if they would ever get a full night's sleep.

Chapter 4

WHEN THE DOOR to her office opened at nine o'clock, Molly greeted the man with a smile and an extended hand. Her smile vanished when she found herself looking at a badge. Holding it was a tall, blond, and extremely handsome man whose blue sports coat matched the blue of his eyes. His white teeth flashed at Molly's surprised gasp.

Mitch Hatch hoped his face didn't show how pleased he was at the pretty, redheaded woman's reaction. His badge was shiny because it was new. This was his first assignment since his promotion to the rank of detective. "Miss Allen, my name is Detective Hatch."

"Excuse me for being surprised. I thought you were my nine o'clock appointment."

"I'm afraid I don't have an appointment, and I apologize for interrupting your morning."

"What can I do for you, Detective?"

"I'd like to ask you a few questions about last night. May I come in?" he asked, flashing his smile.

Molly slowly lowered her extended hand. "Last night? I didn't do anything last night!" she answered, looking puzzled.

"Maybe I asked the wrong question. Let's put it this way; did you go for a walk last night?"

"Yes, I did."

"And did you walk past McGuire's Alley?"

Molly's face relaxed. "Yes, I did. In fact, I walked past it two times last night."

"Two times?" Detective Hatch's eyebrows shot up.

Molly, responding quickly to his reaction, asked, "Is there a law that says I can't do that? Is that why you're here?" she asked, wondering if this was some kind of a joke. "Are you going to arrest me for walking around the block twice last night?"

"Of course not," he smoothed over his response with a quick smile, "but McGuire's Alley was a dangerous place to be last night."

"Dangerous?" Relieved, she smiled back at the handsome detective. "It didn't look dangerous to me, just junky."

"That junky place was the scene of two murders last night," he said quietly.

Molly's smile vanished. "Two murders? Oh dear!"

Detective Hatch watched a series of emotions flash across her face. "These two people," she paused, "would I know them?"

"No, you wouldn't. The victims didn't live in your neighborhood. May I sit down?"

Molly sighed and pushed a pile of maps and brochures off a chair. "Up until now, I've always felt perfectly safe when I walk at night. Guess that's not true anymore."

"I'm wondering," he said, looking closely at the very attractive woman, "why would you choose to walk at night in such a dark area?"

Molly pondered. Just how much detail should she go into describing the problem with her legs? If her own doctor had no idea what she was talking about, what was the use of trying to explain it to the detective? She sure wasn't going to tell this good-looking man about the doctor's referral to a psychiatrist. She looked him straight in the eye and lied.

"I just love to walk at night," she replied, hoping her nose wasn't growing longer. "And sometimes to vary my walk, I do check out McGuire's Alley just to see if he has added anything to his junk pile. Last night I did pause at the entrance but I didn't go in."

"I want to know why you stopped, and what you saw." Detective Hatch watched her face turn thoughtful as she tried to answer his questions. He wondered how much information he should give her. Retaliation in the drug world is sudden and vicious. From what he had found in his computer search, he knew that she was a single woman. The lack of a ring on her left hand confirmed that she wasn't involved in a serious relationship.

"How much longer will this take, Detective Hatch? I have a family coming in any minute, and I have a full morning of scheduled appointments. I don't have much to tell you."

"Then just tell me what you saw last night," he said as he pulled a notebook and pen out of his pocket.

Molly gathered her thoughts. "On my first walk past McGuire's Alley, I thought I heard men's voices. I listened for a bit, but when I didn't hear them again, I just walked on. On my last round, I heard the voices again and I thought I saw a shadow right by the old junked car. I couldn't be sure because most of the streetlights are shot out. And, yes, I did stop and look into the alley but then someone yelled pretty loud and that scared some sense into me. I really didn't see much of anything because it was just too dark. Now, have I answered all your questions?"

"Someone yelled?"

"Yes, and before you ask me about the yell, I'll just tell you that I have no idea. It was just a loud shout," Molly stated.

Detective Hatch's fingers tightened on the pen he was holding. "A name? Could it have been a name?"

Molly shrugged. "It was just a loud shout."

Detective Hatch was about to reply when, after a sharp knock, the door opened to reveal a blonde, pleasant-faced plump woman dressed in a green and red polyester pantsuit. Clara, Molly's secretary, stood in the open doorway and raised her eyebrows in the direction of the good-looking man.

"Miss Allen, your nine o'clock appointment is here. Shall I tell them to wait?"

Standing behind the secretary, Mitch could see a man, a woman, and two children trying to look around her. That wasn't a small undertaking because forty-five year old Clara, who was about that many pounds overweight, blocked the opening. The two children pushed her aside and rushed into the room.

"Kids!" the man scolded sternly.

By this time, a wiry dark-haired boy of about six and his older blonde pigtailed sister had made their way into the office and were looking back and forth between their parents and the man who had been talking with the woman in the red dress.

Detective Hatch turned to Molly. "I won't bother you anymore this morning, but I'll be getting back to you. Good day, Miss Allen." Nodding to the family that was now inside the office, "A good day to all of you, too."

Molly, holding out her hand, smiled up at him. As the detective shook her hand, he was startled when another face flashed in his memory. Puzzled, he held her hand a bit too long and was flustered when she pulled her hand out of his grasp. He backed out the door.

What was all that about? Whatever it was, the feeling he had when he held Miss Allen's hand was making him smile.

Chapter 5

MOLLY INTRODUCED HERSELF to the prospective buyers. Mr. Wise, a banker, was being transferred from Grand Rapids. Dark and small of stature, his direct eye contact, and assertive attitude dared anyone to question his authority; he was a man prepared for battle. The creases in his black pants were sharp, his white shirt was stiffly starched, and his red tie was without blemish.

Today his job was to find the perfect house to please his wife who didn't want to move from Grand Rapids to this small northern Michigan town.

Summer in northern Michigan is a thing of beauty. Molly often joked that this is where God would visit if He took a vacation. During those months, tourists flock to the area. Restaurants that were empty of customers during the winter now have long waiting lines. Hotels and motels on the main entrance coming into town have no vacancies. At the end of summer, the visitors go home. During the winter months, the permanent residents are either the hearty ones who stay behind to curse the snow and the battleship-gray skies, or the ones who use the snow for recreational purposes. To the latter group, a winter sun shining on dazzling white snow is a sight to cherish.

Mrs. Wise, a large woman wearing a shapeless print dress, had obviously been crying. Framing a flaccid face devoid of makeup, her mousy, lank brown hair hung down to her shoulders. It was hard to look past her red-rimmed eyes.

The children, Toby and Susie, pushed their way to stand close to Molly who was explaining that, based on the bank's mortgage approval, she would show them examples of houses in their price range. Mrs. Wise listened half-heartedly, dabbing her eyes with a balled tissue. Her husband made encouraging sounds while they looked at pictures of the house they were to see.

"Mom!" Toby grabbed her hand. "I like that house. Can we buy it?"

With a dismissive sniff, his mother jerked her hand away.

"Mrs. Wise," Molly finally asked, "are you looking for something specific?"

With a resigned sigh, Mrs. Wise replied, "I suppose the houses are fine. Might as well get on with it."

Armed with maps and information, Molly ushered the family through the office past Clara's area. A plate of chocolate chip cookies on her desk caught everyone's eye, but since Clara wasn't around to ask if the cookies were for the taking, Molly didn't offer them.

Mrs. Wise snorted when they pulled into the driveway of the first house. "What person in his right mind would paint a house that color? Looks like something in a baby's diaper."

Toby snickered.

"Paint can be changed," reasoned Mr. Wise. "Would you look at that backyard!"

"Just more grass to mow," sniffed Mrs. Wise. "And since you're never around to do it, it's just one more job for me."

Molly, Mr. Wise, and the two children were out of the car, walking up to the front door when Susie asked, "Why isn't Mom coming?"

Mrs. Wise hadn't moved. "I'm not going," she announced. "I don't like this house, so why should I waste my time looking at it?"

"Mrs. Wise," Molly said in her most soothing voice, "we have an appointment to see this house and the sellers made the effort to be gone. I would ask you to at least go into the house so that I can report back to the sellers that their house was shown." It was becoming apparent that all was not well in 'River City'.

"Well, all right," Mrs. Wise puffed as she worked her way out of the back seat of the car. "Just don't expect me to like it."

The house was quite large with a hardwood hall that ran most of the way through the middle. The children quickly discovered that since the owners were absent, no one was paying any attention to them. As they ran and slid on the slippery floor, Molly watched the parents, waiting for one of them to scold the rowdy children, but neither one paid any attention. Mr. Wise was intent on pointing out good things about the house while Mrs. Wise walked around with a dismissive look on her face. Toby and Susie, seeing they were getting away with their actions, became more boisterous. Finally, Molly corralled them and pointed them toward the door. The two ran past her and raced each other to the car.

At the next house, Mrs. Wise tried her best to come up with a reason not to get out of the car. "Too many windows!" she announced. "Would you look at the size of them? I know we don't have a ladder long enough to reach that high one."

"Dear, now is not the time to worry about windows!" Mr. Wise offered his hand to help his wife work her way out of the back seat.

"Harrumph!" exploded Mrs. Wise. "That's easy for you to say! You're never around, so I guess it would be me that needs to worry about it."

Shaking off her husband's hand, she turned back to the car. "I don't really want to go in," she grumbled. "Can I stay out in the car? I know I'm not going to like this house."

The curtain at a kitchen window fluttered, and a face appeared. "Mrs. Wise," Molly said in a controlled voice; enough was enough, "See that woman at the window?"

"Yes," answered Mrs. Wise, "what about her?"

"We have an appointment to see this house. That woman, knowing her house is going to be shown to a buyer, probably cleaned, vacuumed, and dusted for a couple of hours." Molly watched Mrs. Wise digest this information.

"You're telling me that I need to go in. I get it," grumbled Mrs. Wise as she joined the rest of her family.

Agents routinely tell their sellers that it's best for them not to be home during a showing. Unfortunately, these particular owners felt the need to follow Molly and her buyers around; they wanted to make sure none of the good points went unnoticed. This gave Toby and Susie a chance to be alone.

Their house in a Grand Rapids suburb was a ranch and didn't have a second story, so the long carpeted staircase fascinated the children. It took only a few times of running up and down the stairs until Toby discovered he could flatten his body and slide down as if he were on a sled. Susie glanced at her parents, expecting to see some sign of disapproval. When she saw they weren't paying any attention, she ran to the top of the stairs and came flying down on her back.

The sellers, hearing the commotion, looked at Molly with displeasure. She waited a few seconds to see if either parent noticed, but Mr. Wise was still intent on trying to get his dejected wife interested in the house. Molly rushed to the bottom of the stairs just in time to straddle Susie as she came to a sliding stop.

"Let's go upstairs and see the bedrooms," Molly said, trying to distract them. "Want to pick your favorite one?"

Susie jumped up and yelled, "I get dibs on the biggest one!" and ran up the stairs past Toby who, for some reason, was not taking her up on the bedroom challenge. In fact, he wasn't moving at all. The small whimper that started at the back of his throat grew into an hysterical cry, "Help! My head's stuck! I can't get it out!" Toby had wedged his head between the spindles of the stair rail.

Mrs. Wise came running. Taking charge, she calmed Toby down as she maneuvered his stuck head.

"I think we should call the fire department!" the seller's wife cried, wringing her hands.

"They'll just saw through the rails," her husband said quietly. "Do you want that?"

Toby had cried so hard he was wet with sweat and his ears stuck out like red tomatoes on either side of his head.

"Do you have anything that's slippery, like petroleum jelly?" Mr. Wise asked. "Let's try that before we call anyone."

The owner of the house came running with a large jar and, after enough of it was rubbed over his head and throbbing ears, Mrs. Wise succeeded in removing Toby's head from between the rails. His sobs became hiccups that soon turned into quiet breathing. The exhausted boy had fallen asleep in his mother's arms.

Molly was both embarrassed and angry; things like this were not supposed to happen. She apologized profusely to the sellers and made a mental note to have Clara send flowers.

MOLLY HERDED THE FAMILY out the front door while heaping apologetic words on the grim-faced sellers. She was sure she would be hearing from the listing office. The sellers were probably already calling their agent.

A wave of exhaustion overwhelmed her as she started the car. The consequence of sleeping only a few hours the night before was catching up with her. Stopping for a red light, she closed her eyes and rested her forehead on the steering wheel. The silence in the car was hanging so heavy she could feel it. Since climbing into the car, the Wise family had not said a word.

Honking horns jolted her awake; she had done it again. Falling asleep while waiting for a traffic light to change was happening to her frequently. She stomped on the accelerator and sped away from the intersection.

Mrs. Wise offered no objections about the last house when Molly pulled into the driveway. The Wise family walked through the house without much enthusiasm, said nothing about it, got back into the car and quietly rode back to the office.

Once in the parking lot, Molly surveyed the family. The tension between the parents was obvious. Today's house hunting had brought some major problems to the surface.

Mr. Wise was sitting in the passenger side of the front seat. He had started today's house search with confidence, but now he looked like a defeated man. Mrs. Wise, in the back seat with the children, appeared weary and defensive. Susie was huddled in the window seat, feeling anxious about the strain between her parents. Toby, oblivious to the family drama, squirmed closer to his mother and announced, "I'm hungry!"

Seeing a chance to give the couple privacy, Molly said, "You two can talk about the houses we saw today while I run in and see if any of those cookies are left."

When Molly was away from the car, Mr. Wise said, "I know this transfer is hard on you, dear, but did you see anything at all that you liked this morning?"

Mrs. Wise leaned toward her husband and said harshly, "Nothing we saw even comes close to what you're making us leave in Grand Rapids. Miss Allen claims she showed us the best of what we can afford here. I will *not* accept that!"

"But I have to take the transfer or I'll lose my job!" Mr. Wise looked stunned. "The front office has made it clear to me! Too many younger men are willing to move where the company wants to send them. If I don't take the transfer, I'll be let go. At my age, I can't afford for that to happen!"

Mrs. Wise took a deep breath and made a decision; now was the time to say all the words she had been holding back. For a long while, she had been unhappy with her marriage and the prospect of the transfer was the last straw. "I'm going to say something that you probably won't want to hear. Please don't think this is a hasty decision."

Mr. Wise, puzzled at this unexpected turn of events, spun around to look at his wife. "What don't I want to hear?"

"You can come here with your precious promotion and live by yourself," Mrs. Wise said in a flat voice. "The kids and I are staying in Grand Rapids."

"Tell me you aren't serious!" he gasped. "I can't believe you said that."

"I said it, and I mean it." Mrs. Wise's finger poked him in the shoulder. "I've had enough of your long work hours. It's always been your job ahead of me and the kids."

"But I only work those long hours because I want to be a good provider for my family!" Mr. Wise gulped for air. "I want all of you to have the best of everything. That's why I work so hard." His eyes, full of unshed tears, pled with her to understand as he reached back and took her hand. "It's always been for you!"

"So you say," she exclaimed, pulling her hand away, "but where were you all the times I needed you when the kids were sick, or when I wanted a bit of relief from being constantly stuck at home, or when I wanted to have an adult conversation at the end of the day? You were always too tired from your 'hard day' at work. As if my days were all sunshine and roses! You never tried to understand even when I explained it to you. I'm telling you now that I'm not putting up with it anymore. Just take your promotion and leave me alone. I probably won't even notice you're gone!" she paused, took a deep breath and her voice softened as she added, "I've wanted to say this to you for a long time, and sitting here in a salesperson's car in a strange town is probably not the best place to be saying it, but I want out of this so-called marriage!"

Mr. Wise's mouth dropped open at this new unexpected turn of events. He had thought that Toby's getting his head stuck in the railing would be the most disastrous thing that happened in this house-hunting venture; he had never anticipated the end of the morning would also be the end of his marriage.

Toby had nodded off during his parent's conversation, but Susie was listening intently. She understood what they were yelling about.

MOLLY RUSHED INTO the office and slid to a stop by the cookie plate on Clara's desk.

"Thank goodness there are cookies left! Oh yes, something else, remind me to give you the address where I want you to send some flowers." When Clara's mouth opened to ask why, Molly held up her hand to stop her. "There's a story attached to all of this but I don't have time to tell you."

She could feel the strained atmosphere when she got back to the car; the chocolate chip cookies didn't improve the mood. Mr. Wise cleared his throat. "Miss Allen, it won't be necessary for us to go to your office. We're tired and we want to start our trip back, but thank you for all you've done for us. I'll call you tomorrow."

Rejection. The nemesis of every salesperson in the world.

Molly had a feeling that nothing good was going to come from her morning's work. She had known what to expect when she chose to follow her dad into this business. As a child, he had shared with her the stories of why he missed important events like birthday parties and school events to work with buyers that, more likely than not, never bought anything.

As Molly watched the family drive away, she became aware of that familiar rejected feeling, accompanied by the suspicion that she'd never see any of them again.

Chapter 6

MITCH HATCH PULLED his coat tighter to his body and fastened the top button. A cold wind had picked up, blowing the fall leaves around the bench where he had been sitting for the past twenty minutes. Before he had dressed for work this morning, he hadn't checked the weather report. Shivering, he was regretting his choices when the person he was waiting for walked by his bench.

Without looking at Mitch, the person spoke quietly. "I'll be behind the oak tree by the park entrance."

Mitch waited a few minutes then casually got up and followed. Since they always met at night, all Mitch knew about his contact was that he was an outstanding recruit at the Police Academy and an unknown face on the street. It was dark behind the tree. He had never really gotten a good look at the guy who went by his gang name, Zeek. At that moment, a car turned into the park, throwing light through the thick foliage. The undercover agent quickly stepped back into the trees, but not before Mitch caught a brief glimpse. For the second time today, the face he had just seen reminded him of someone. He remembered that he had experienced the same feeling this morning when he was talking with Miss Allen.

"Anything new to tell me?" whispered Mitch.

"I'm afraid the neighborhood kids are in over their heads," the voice answered. "I was planted in their group when petty thefts and shooting out streetlights were the worst things they did. But now, three men have shown up from Chicago and somehow connected themselves to our boys. One guy has taken over and he's using the boys to run errands for him."

"What about the two murders? Did the three guys do that?" asked Mitch.

"Yes. The one that is the leader is a foul-mouthed character called Sammy the Grunt," the man whispered.

"Sammy the what?"

"Sammy the Grunt. Cleaning up after a bloody job is called grunt work."

"Besides this grunt guy, who are the other two?" asked Mitch.

"I don't know their last names, but their first names are Clarence and Albert. However, I've only seen those two a couple of times. Sammy keeps them busy running errands for him. But, from what I hear, Clarence is a simpleton and the rest of the gang is puzzled why Sammy puts up with him. The other one is Albert who tells some pretty tall stories."

"Has anyone talked about the two victims? We're running their fingerprints, but we haven't come up with identification yet."

"From what I've been able to pick up, the two dead ones were old associates of Sammy. They followed him here from Chicago, knowing that Sammy's usually into something, and they wanted to cash in on it."

"Why did Sammy come here to begin with?" whispered Mitch. "This is not a logical town for the likes of him."

"What I know is just what I've been able to put together from scattered conversations; I can't afford to bring attention to myself by asking questions."

"So? What have you learned?" Mitch asked.

"From what I can gather, Sammy had a cellmate some years back who dreamed of coming back to what he called 'God's country'. The cellmate made northern Michigan sound like heaven, and Sammy wanted to check it out. Their real destination is a town in the middle of the state, the drug hub between Chicago and Detroit. The Feds have their informants planted in that town, and I wouldn't be surprised if they have their eyes on Sammy, too. I don't think he planned to stay around very long, but he just couldn't resist using his Chicago connections to spread his poison in our area. Unfortunately, he found some takers."

"What's he up to now?" whispered Mitch.

"Sammy is wild. Someone was seen near McGuire's Alley when the murders happened, and Sammy wants that person found and permanently eliminated."

"I interviewed a walker this morning," Mitch found himself smiling at the memory of the woman in the red dress. "She claims she heard someone yelling, but saw nothing because it was too dark."

"She telling the truth?"

"For her sake, I hope she is," Mitch replied fervently.

The man inched closer to Mitch and whispered. "Tell that woman to knock off walking at night in that neighborhood. Sammy is determined to find out who she is and he's posting lookouts. Hell, I'm one of them tonight. Anybody who comes near the area will be a target."

Mitch peered into the darkness, trying to see the face of his informant. The man stepped back, but not before Mitch again had the feeling that there was something vaguely familiar about the guy.

"I'll get in contact with you the usual way if I need to." With that, the man disappeared into the park.

Mitch's eyes squinted, trying to see the right button on his cell phone; he had put Miss Allen's office phone number on speed dial. What was the chance that anyone would be at the office this late? He could hear it ringing and was about to give up when someone picked up the phone.

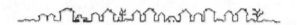

Chapter 7

MOLLY REFLECTED ON the morning's events. She had felt the animosity between the husband and wife when she had returned to the car with the cookies.

The afternoon passed quietly while Molly and Clara did paperwork on pending sales. Molly noticed that Clara was filing her scarlet nails. Her head was bent to the task and Molly got a glimpse of a blonde dye job gone wrong. Black roots were showing in the midst of tightly permed orange hair. Across her ample bosom, buttons were straining to hold closed the jacket of her red pantsuit.

Molly smiled to herself thinking about her dad when he had trouble buttoning his pants. "My pants fit too soon!" is what she fondly remembered him saying.

"Clara, how would you like the rest of the day off? Looks like you're caught up."

"You kidding?" Clara dropped the file. "I can go home early? I'll try not to slam the door on the way out! See you tomorrow!" she called to Molly as she grabbed her purse and slammed the door on her way out. Molly, amused, shook her head.

Molly had hired Clara Clark after she'd sold her a small condominium at the edge of town. Clara got the short end of the stick in a messy divorce when her husband's lawyer turned out to be meaner and more aggressive than her own lawyer was. After the dust had settled, she was left dazed, broke, disillusioned, and deeply depressed. Molly, watching a good woman turn into a bitter wreck, offered her a few hours of work a week just to get her out of the condo. Clara attacked the office work with all the pent-up vengeance she felt for her slime-ball husband and his thirty-year-old bimbo. The part-time job became a full-time job.

The silent and empty office was a welcome relief to Molly after the frustrating day. Exhaustion rolled over her body. Thinking about gathering up her purse and driving home took too much effort. Instead, she laid her head down on her desk and immediately fell asleep.

Much later, the ringing phone woke her. Lifting her head from the desk, she looked around in confusion. The phone was on the fifth ring when she gathered her wits together and answered it.

"Hello."

"Miss Allen?"

"Yes," she managed to get out. "How can I help you?"

"Miss Allen, this is Detective Hatch."

Molly jerked her head up and wiped drool off her chin.

"Oh, hello, Detective Hatch. You caught me still here at the office catching up on some paper work," she lied.

"Are you all right? You sound a bit groggy."

"Probably a cold coming on, nothing more." She faked a cough. "What are you calling about?"

"I'm sorry to bother you so late in the evening, but I really need to discuss something with you."

She shook her head, trying to wake up. "I don't know what you have to discuss with me, Detective. I've already told you everything I know about last night."

"I understand that," he answered patiently. "What I have to say to you concerns your safety."

"My safety? I don't understand!" Molly pushed back her chair and stood up.

"We believe that the two murders are connected to three men from Chicago." Mitch was talking slowly, wanting to be sure Molly understood the danger she was in. "The leader, whose name is Sammy the Grunt, is quite convinced that someone was walking by at the time of the murders. I believe that someone was you and that you saw and heard more than you are saying."

"But I didn't see anything!" she wailed.

"Sammy seems quite willing to permanently remove that someone if he could figure out who it is." He paused when he heard her gasp. "I know for a fact that he's posting lookouts around the clock. At this point, I would imagine they'll grab anyone near that place, day or night. I want you to realize the danger you're in. These three men aren't to be taken lightly." He waited for her response.

"Are you there, Miss Allen?" He knew she was still there because he could hear her breathing. "Do you understand what I just told you?"

Molly was still groggy from her nap. Her neck hurt and the arm that had cradled her head on the desk was sound asleep.

"Let me get this straight. You're telling me that somewhere there's a 'Grunt' Sammy who would kill me if he could find me?" she asked, finding it hard to put it into words.

"Yes, unfortunately, that's what I'm telling you," he said as gently as he could.

Someone wanted to kill her? Her heart beat wildly and her mouth went dry. "What are the chances that he'll find out it was me?" she croaked. Her hands were shaking and her voice quivered. All the while she was talking she was frantically looking around the dark office, wondering if there was a safe hiding place in the building.

Mitch could hear the terror in her voice. Since he had met her just once, he was surprised at the strength of his feelings; he definitely didn't want anything bad happening to her. There was no name for what he had felt when he shook her hand, but he was still smiling about it. "Is there some place you could stay tonight?" he asked. "I don't think it's safe for you to go home."

Her mind went blank; then she thought of Clara. The condo she had sold her had an extra bedroom and she was sure Clara would take her in for the night.

"I have a secretary who will let me stay with her; I'll call her right away," Molly said, her voice unsteady. "I'm having trouble believing someone wants to kill me."

"I'm sorry that I upset you, but I had to make sure you understood the situation," he said, wishing he were there to comfort her.

"Oh, I understand all right!" she said, her voice trembling. "Since no one has ever threatened to kill me before, maybe I'm over-reacting, but I'm terrified!"

"Make that call, Miss Allen, and my advice to you is to stay with your secretary until I tell you it's safe to go home," he said quietly. "Good night, Miss Allen."

"Good night, Detective Hatch."

Stunned, Molly sat at her desk, unable to move. Someone wanted her dead? The very thought of a world without her was unthinkable. Death was what happened to other people, not to her. Her shaking hand had almost made it to the phone when it rang; she screamed.

"Hello?" she croaked. "Hello?"

Click.

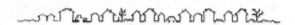

Chapter 8

TOM ALLEN, his red hair tucked securely under his hat, was glad the streetlights weren't working. It was a dark night, and for that, Tom was thankful. He pulled the hat down over his ears, buttoned his coat against the chill of the night, and looked for a secluded place to spend the next four hours.

Keeping his mouth shut and his eyes open, Tom gathered details of the activities within the group. The local drug supplier had chosen McGuire's Alley as the ideal place to stash the drugs for a later pick-up. To transfer the drugs without arousing suspicion, the dealer's young son came up with the idea of hiding them in the vegetable bin of the junked refrigerator. Not wanting to blow Tom's cover, a police raid was delayed until they had more information on the supplier. Since the drugs were coming across state lines, the DEA was involved.

It was a good plan, but Sammy's old buddies from Chicago found the hiding place before the crack-down. Sammy's catching them stealing the drugs was what Molly had heard on her late walk. She would have heard much more had she lingered because the two thieves hadn't died quietly.

Ever since the murders, Sammy had posted boys in the neighborhood ready to report any lone walkers. Tonight, Tom was assigned to the area around McGuire's Alley. After finding an easy-to-climb tree, he spent the next four hours hoping there were no walkers tonight.

All was quiet on the dark street. Tom suspected that a double murder would keep most people indoors for a few days. It seemed like a nice neighborhood, too nice for activity like this. Then he remembered his mother telling him that his sister, Molly, had bought a house. He hadn't paid much attention and his mom hadn't mentioned where the house was, but now, Tom thought about Molly's late night walking. He didn't quite understand why she did this, but for as long as Tom could remember, Molly walked at night. He would check with Mom tomorrow. For Molly's sake, he hoped this wasn't her neighborhood and that she wasn't the walker.

The four hours of his watch passed slowly; there were no walkers tonight. He was about to slide down the trunk when a moving shadow crawled out of the junked car and disappeared into the night.

Chapter 9

CLARA WAS WATCHING out the window when Molly's car careened into the parking lot. She was puzzled when she saw Molly reach into the back seat and pull out a small suitcase.

"Girlfriend, you need a suitcase for an overnighter?" she called as she stepped out on her porch. "I thought this was going to be a pajama party!"

"I stopped at the mall on the way here and picked up enough clothes for the next few days," Molly explained as she slammed the car door. "Let's go inside, and I'll tell you what's going on."

Following her into the small condo, Clara watched while Molly headed for the spare bedroom. She was waiting to see Molly's reaction when she opened the door and found the bedroom wasn't furnished. In fact, the only thing in it was a sleeping bag. Clara had managed to move only a few pieces of furniture out of her beautiful house before her louse of a husband and his bimbo had changed the locks.

Finding the room empty, Molly shrugged. "I wish having to sleep on the floor was the worst of my problems." She set her suitcase down. "I'm starved. Any chance there is something to eat? Feed me, and I'll tell you what's going on."

Molly wasn't disappointed when she walked into Clara's kitchen. The table, which sported a bright red cloth and place mats, had a delicious-smelling casserole as its centerpiece.

After filling their plates, Clara asked, "Does this have anything to do with that good- looking man who came to your office this morning? I love eye candy with my morning coffee, and he sure fit that bill!"

"That wasn't eye candy you were looking at. That was a cop. Well, I should say detective, because that is who he is, Detective Hatch."

Clara cocked her head to one side and gave her green-eyed boss a speculative look. "Now, girl, what have you done that would bring a detective to your office? You have your work and that's about it. I didn't mention a social life, because you don't have one. So what did you do?" she teased, "Sing too loud in church?"

"I wish," Molly replied. She looked at Clara and wondered if she would understand what she was about to tell her and not think she was weird. "Clara, I'm going to tell you something that I haven't told very many people. It's what I do at night that got me into the mess that I'm in now."

Clara's eyes widened. "You're a vampire?"

Molly, stunned by Clara's question, finally grinned at her secretary. "A vampire? What a novel thought! No, Clara, I'm not going to bite your neck tonight while you're sleeping!"

"Thank you, God!" Clara rolled her eyes. "So, if you're not a vampire, what's your problem?"

"I walk."

"You walk?" Clara's eyebrows went up so high they almost met her tightly permed orange hair.

"Yes, I walk. At night, my legs seem to have a life of their own; I can't keep them still. They have this relentless need to move, so I walk."

"Okay, so you walk." Clara thought for a moment and then asked, "Why would walking bring eye candy to your door this morning?"

"Last night there was a double murder in my neighborhood."

Clara drew a sharp intake of breath. Molly waited for her to close her mouth.

"Seems the bad guys saw someone in the area where the murders happened." Molly continued. "I was walking last night at the right time and the right place...maybe I should say the wrong time and the wrong place, because now they're trying to find me. They think I heard and saw something that would tie them to the murders."

Clara dropped the hand that was covering her open mouth. "Does that detective think you're in danger?"

"Yes, he does. He says they would think nothing of doing away with me permanently if they thought I was a potential problem."

"Wait one minute," Clara cried, "does 'permanent' mean what I think it means?"

Molly shivered. "Yes! I'm having trouble believing someone wants to kill me. And, get this; the guy who's the leader is called Sammy the Grunt. Can you believe that?"

"Sammy the Grunt? For real? "

Molly nodded.

"How did this grunt guy discover that you were the walker?"

Molly's voice shook. "Maybe I'm not the one he's looking for. Maybe someone else was out that night, but so was I. Some neighbors know me as the 'nightwalker'. We don't exchange names, but I'm sure they know which house is mine. All they had to do was to point out my house to the detective. City records would tell him who owned it. I don't know how he found where I work, though."

"If the detective had no problem finding where you work, what makes you think Sammy can't do the same? What's the detective doing about this?"

"There's an undercover man who's keeping him informed. He told Detective Hatch that Sammy has posted a lookout on my block. It was the detective's insistence that I stay out of the neighborhood for awhile."

"How about staying out forever, or at least until this murder gets solved! This is awful!" Clara cried. "Do you think you can even go back to work? Do you need police protection?"

"Maybe, but it's too early in the game to plan that far ahead," Molly answered. "Let's just get through tonight."

Just thinking about getting through the night made Molly cringe. What was she going to do about her damn legs in this small condo? How could she walk when there was no place to walk?

Then she remembered some sample medication the doctor had reluctantly given her the last time she had cried in his office while describing her tortured nights.

Before crawling into the sleeping bag, Molly rummaged through her purse and found the sample pills.

Tonight would be her very first sleepover. All her life she had shied away from pajama parties, not knowing how she could handle the need to move her legs at night in a strange house. She would listen with envy when, the next day, her friends would be giggling about how they had pretended to be asleep when the dad of the family thundered into their room. The description they gave of him standing there with his hair in spikes and, without his glasses, squinting eyes, made her sad because she hadn't been there to see it.

Tonight, with a feeling of dread, Molly laid the pills aside and reluctantly crawled into the sleeping bag.

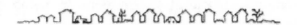

Chapter 10

THE HOUSE WAS DARK when Mitch pulled into Miss Allen's driveway the next morning. He smiled with anticipation as he rang the doorbell.

When he had last seen Miss Allen, her red hair had been piled on top of her head. He hoped that, when she answered the door this morning, she would be coming straight from bed, and her hair would be rumpled and down around her shoulders. Seeing her green eyes and dimples would be nice, too.

When a neighbor had pointed out her house, Mitch had gone to the city records to see who owned it. He found that 'Molly Allen, a single female', owned it.

Three jabs at the doorbell brought no response. Since he couldn't hear the doorbell ring, he deduced that it wasn't working. When pounding on the door didn't produce any results, he concluded that Molly had taken his advice and spent the night elsewhere.

Pulling out his cell phone, he called her office. He figured no one would be there at this early hour, but he would leave a message for her to pick up later.

"Miss Allen, this is Detective Hatch. Please call me at your earliest convenience. My cell number is 555-0967."

IT WAS EARLY MORNING when Clara woke to a quiet condo. She lay there stretching until she suddenly remembered she had an overnight guest.

Jumping out of bed, she ran to the kitchen to make coffee and a simple breakfast. She wondered if Molly intended to go to work today. If the detective could find out where Molly lived and worked, Clara reasoned, why couldn't the bad guys do the same?

She skidded to a stop at the kitchen's entrance. There, with her red hair spread over the paper place mat from last night's dinner was Molly, fast asleep.

"Molly, are you all right?" asked Clara, shaking her gently.

Groaning, Molly lifted her head, the paper mat stuck to the side of her face. She rubbed her neck and rolled her head back and forth. Clara reached over and removed the mat from her cheek. "Have a bad night?"

"You might say that," Molly muttered.

"You must be worried sick about the threat to your life," Clara sympathized as she sat down. "No wonder you couldn't sleep! You should have wakened me."

"Why should you lose sleep just because I can't sleep? And yes, knowing that someone wants to kill me didn't make sleep come easy, but that's not what kept me awake." Molly rubbed her eyes. "I feel like someone hit me over the head." Sitting up, she massaged her stiff neck.

"I'm so sorry you had to sleep on the floor!" Clara said, too embarrassed to look Molly in the eye. "Sometimes in my imagination I have my fingers around the neck of my slime-ball husband!"

Molly laughed. "Hey, that sleeping bag was pretty comfortable, but don't let me stop you from strangling him if it makes you feel better!"

"So, if it wasn't the sleeping bag or the bad guy who wants to kill you, what was it that kept you from sleeping?"

"My legs. When they say walk, I walk," Molly sighed. "They have a life of their own, it seems."

"I guess you should have sold me a bigger condo. There's not much walking room in this one."

"You don't need a bigger condo, Clara. This one suits you just fine."

"So how did you end up in my kitchen?"

"I gave up trying to walk about two o'clock so I took some pills I've been carrying around in my purse. The last time I cried in the doctor's office about not being able to sleep, he gave me some samples."

"I take it they didn't help your legs," Clara said looking concerned. "If they had, I wouldn't have found you asleep with your head on my kitchen table this morning."

"Hey, don't knock your kitchen table! No, the pills just made me dizzy and nauseated. I ended up walking around for a while before I finally sat down and I guess I must have slept some. What a house guest I've turned out to be!"

Clara jumped up. "How does a cup of coffee sound right now?"

"How about several cups?"

"Are you planning on going into work today, or are you afraid enough to stay out of sight for a bit?" Clara's voice loomed over the banging of pots and pans. "I'm making eggs. Is poached okay?"

"You're the cook; surprise me!" Molly paused, and then added, "I really don't have much going on today, but I probably should call the office and listen to the messages just to make sure. I haven't heard a word from the Wise family, but I didn't really expect to. I'd bet money that I'll never hear from them again."

After finishing breakfast, she used Clara's kitchen phone to call in for her messages. Most of them were from title and mortgage companies with last minute updates on the progress of sold properties. She had a few closings coming up, but there was nothing urgent that she needed to take care of today. One call was nothing but heavy breathing; probably someone calling a wrong number...or maybe Clara has a secret admirer. She would have to remember to tease her about that.

The last call was from Detective Hatch. Molly looked puzzled as she listened to the message. Why was he asking her to call him? "Clara, I need to write down a phone number," she said, motioning to her secretary. She replayed the message and, listening carefully, wrote down a number, and hung up.

"Clara, Detective Hatch wants me to call him but I'm not making a call to anyone until I get the cotton out of my head."

SEVERAL CUPS OF COFFEE LATER, Molly's head felt clear enough to make the call.

"It's not fair," she groaned, as she searched through her pajama pockets. "I have a hangover but I don't remember the party! Where is that piece of paper? I wrote the detective's number on something."

"Here it is! Want me to read you the number?" Clara teased. "I don't think your eyes are focused yet. I can also dial it for you!"

Molly lunged for the paper. "Come on! I'm not in that bad shape!"

"You aren't in good shape either!" laughed Clara, tauntingly waving the piece of paper.

"I give up. Read me the number, please."

The phone was picked up on the second ring.

"Detective Hatch?"

She hadn't given her name, but a sensation in his heart told him who it was. Surprised, he took a deep breath to steady its beat and asked, "Miss Allen?"

"Good morning! I'm returning your call."

"Are you in your office?" he asked.

"No. I took your advice and spent the night with my secretary. You might remember her from yesterday."

"Yes, I do. Have you had breakfast yet?"

"Nothing more than coffee," she lied as she wiped the last bit of poached egg from her lips.

Clara's eyebrows rose as she wagged her finger at Molly.

"Are you familiar with the Omelet Shop on Front Street?"

"Yes, I am."

"Could you meet me there, say, in an hour?" Mitch held his breath, waiting for an answer.

Clara rolled her eyes while trying to hear both ends of the conversation.

"I think I can manage that," Molly replied.

Clara clapped her hands.

Molly took the time to stick out her tongue at Clara before saying to Detective Hatch, "I'll be there. Bye!"

WITH A TOWEL WRAPPED around her head, Molly ran from the shower to the bedroom. She rummaged through her suitcase trying to remember what she had bought yesterday at the mall. Being afraid to go to her own house in case the bad guys had figured out where she lived, she'd grabbed a few outfits off the racks along with some other essentials.

EVELYN ALLEN HARPER

Clara stood in the doorway watching Molly toss the contents of the suitcase onto the floor. "Having trouble picking out what you want to wear to meet Mr. Eye Candy, are you?"

"Quit calling him that!" Molly said crossly.

She was going through the pile for the second time, not quite sure how she wanted to dress for her post-breakfast breakfast. "I could use a little help here."

"About time you asked for my help! That green cashmere sweater is the same color as your eyes. Wear that."

"Really? My eyes are *that* color?"

"You should try looking into the mirror sometime, Molly. You have beautiful eyes."

"Go on now!" She held the sweater up and looked at herself in the mirror. "Will these jeans look all right with it?"

"Jeans go with everything. Now what are you going to do with your hair? You aren't going to go all prissy and pull it off your face, are you?"

"Are you a fashion critic now?" teased Molly. "What do you want me to do with my hair?"

"Nothing," Clara answered. "Just go natural and see what happens."

52

Chapter 11

DETECTIVE MITCH HATCH sat at a back table facing the door. He wanted to be able to see Molly when she arrived. Since yesterday, he had trouble getting her out of his head. The memory of her green-eyes and her dimpled grin had haunted him as he drifted to sleep.

Molly was breathing hard. Putting herself together and getting to the Omelet Shop in one hour had been a challenge. She stopped and looked over the room, finally spotting Mitch at a back table. He hadn't yet seen her so she had time to study him as she walked toward the table. Today he was dressed casually in a summer-sky-blue turtleneck sweater that matched his eyes. Clara was right; Mitch definitely was eye candy.

He stood up when she reached the table. "Good morning, Miss Allen."

"Please, call me Molly."

"I will if you'll call me Mitch," he said, smiling broadly.

"Well, then, good morning, Mitch!" Molly returned his smile.

"I've ordered coffee, but I can change that if you'd prefer something else."

"Coffee is fine. I'm having trouble clearing my head this morning, and I think a few more cups might do it."

"Aren't you feeling well?"

She noticed the genuine concern in his voice. "I'm still fuzzy-brained from a sleeping pill I took last night, but other than that, I'm fine," she assured him.

53

"Let's place our orders," he said as the waitress approached their table, "and then we can talk while we're waiting for our food."

When the waitress walked away, Molly looked across the table at Mitch and immediately dropped her gaze. She wished Clara hadn't named him Mr. Eye Candy because now she was having trouble looking at him. Slowly, lifting her eyes off the menu, she studied his face. When it struck her that he looked a lot like Ken, Barbie's boyfriend, she grinned, thinking she had to remember to tell that to Clara.

Mitch was looking at Molly, aware that his heart had just skipped a beat. Yesterday her red hair had been severely pulled back and piled on top of her head. Today it was falling in waves down to her shoulders. Her green sweater made her eyes sparkle, and the dimples, one on each side of her mouth, were deep because she was smiling. It took some effort for him to pull his eyes away. He cleared his throat. "Uh, how's the real estate business these days?" he asked.

She smiled, raised her eyes, and found herself looking at Mr. Eye Candy. "Can't complain," she muttered, looking down.

"I see a lot of your signs around town," Mitch tried again.

"Yes," she said, and dared to raise her eyes. When Ken the doll looked back at her, she squirmed and looked away.

Mitch was disappointed. This was not the breakfast he had envisioned. Molly hadn't seemed this uncomfortable when he interviewed her yesterday. He wondered what was making her so reserved today, but that thought was interrupted by the waitress placing their food on the table.

Molly studied her plate, closed her eyes, leaned over it, and took a deep breath.

Puzzled, Mitch was wondering if Molly was invoking some kind of blessing on her breakfast when she blushed, opened her eyes and said, "I can't believe I did that!"

"Molly, believe me, you don't ever have to apologize for giving thanks before a meal. I would have joined you if you had said something."

"I-I-I wasn't praying," Molly stuttered.

Without saying a word, Mitch's eyes questioned her statement.

"I was smelling the bacon."

He was momentarily stunned by her unexpected answer. "Smelling the bacon?"

Molly's face was red. "Yes, I was smelling the bacon."

Seeing that Molly was truly in distress, Mitch closed his eyes, leaned over his plate and inhaled.

Molly choked on a chuckle. When he opened his eyes and his face was serious, her hand flew to her mouth. "Are you going to tell me you were praying?" she asked in alarm.

"Just smelling the bacon!" he replied, his blue eyes twinkling with amusement.

"You almost had me there," laughed Molly, relieved that the man across from her was now neither Mr. Eye Candy nor Ken; he was just Mitch.

Mitch wondered where this bacon-patter was going, but he didn't care; Molly had relaxed. "I'm curious. Does the smell of bacon remind you of something or somebody?" he asked.

She looked up at him with a dimpled smile. "Like what?"

"Uh, well, how about memories of breakfast at home with your mom in the kitchen and your dad with a newspaper in front of his face?"

"Could be," Molly grinned. "And what about your memories?"

Mitch leaned back in his chair and enjoyed looking at his breakfast companion. "Most Sundays I have brunch with my mom and dad. The smell of frying bacon that hits my nose when I walk in the door...well, I know I'm home."

Feeling relieved that Mr. Eye Candy and Ken had vanished, Molly, with laughter in her voice, proclaimed, "In my humble opinion, the smell of frying bacon is what turns a house into a home."

Mitch chuckled. "I think you should print that statement on your business card."

"I don't know about business cards, but it does sound like something you'd see stitched on a pillow."

"Can you sew?" he asked.

"No, and I even have trouble with buttons," she confessed. "But that's where my secretary, Clara, comes in handy."

"Your secretary sews on your buttons?" Mitch chortled. "If a man asked his secretary to do that for him, she'd haul him up on some kind of sexual harassment!"

"Well, not *my* Clara," Molly declared, scraping her plate clean. "We have an understanding." Molly looked down at her empty plate, surprised that she had finished her second breakfast. An empty plate meant breakfast with Mitch was almost over.

Their eyes met and locked. When Mitch looked away, Molly realized she had been holding her breath.

"Time to get down to business," he said in a husky voice.

Molly blinked and then nodded. Mitch reached across the table and touched her hand.

"Remember I said I had a plant inside the local gang? Sammy the Grunt is using those boys as lookouts, watching for the walker. My guy is one of them. He was about to end his shift when he saw someone crawl out of that old junked car in McGuire's Alley."

"What?" she asked, distracted by his touch.

"You didn't hear what I just said?"

Molly took a deep breath and the dazed look in her eyes disappeared. "Yes, I heard," she said. "You said someone was hiding in that old car. That's hard to believe! There's not much left of that car to hide in," she managed to say. "How come the police didn't find him?"

"From the outside, the rusty trunk looks like it had collapsed. In fact, it had. Whoever squeezed his body into that small space can't be very big. By the way, we don't believe he was connected to Sammy."

"So then who is he?" Molly asked.

"We don't know," Mitch said, "but if he had been one of Sammy's men, he would have gone with them."

"Do you think he might have seen what happened?"

"Yes, we think he's a witness. He knows he's a dead man if Sammy the Grunt gets hold of him."

"Is there really a guy named that?" Molly gave Mitch a questioning look. "It just sounds so ridiculous."

"Unfortunately, there is. The story is that he got that name for doing all the clean-up work after a hit. When one member referred to it as grunt work, the name stuck. Anyhow, it had been quiet for so long in the alley that the man thought it was safe to come out of the trunk."

"So you're telling me," Molly said, speaking slowly, "that somewhere there's a witness to a double murder running around my neighborhood?"

"I'm afraid so, Molly. But Sammy doesn't know there was anyone hiding in the car. As far as he's concerned, *you* are the witness."

Molly, her face serious, asked quietly, "So I'm still in danger?"

Mitch fought the urge to reach across the table and hug her. "Until we find the witness that can finger the murderers, you're going to have to lie low."

"Lie low like not going to work?" she protested. "I have a business to run!"

"Is your business as important as your life?" Mitch tapped her hand. "I'll say it again. Sammy the Grunt will do anything to find and silence the person he thinks saw him do the killings."

"But it wasn't me!" Molly wailed.

"You and I know that, but Sammy doesn't. And for that, I'm sorry," Mitch said as he watched her face crumble.

"So, what do I do? Do you think I'm safe at my secretary's condo?" croaked Molly as she pulled her hand free. "Will I be putting Clara in danger if I stay there?"

"I just know you can't go home," Mitch said, surprised at how empty his hand felt. "It was easy for me to find the house of the night walker; that's what your neighbors call you. The city records told me who owned the house and the man who pointed out your house also told me he had seen you putting real estate signs in your car."

"I was wondering how you found where I work," she said quietly.

"Because I have quick access to city records, I found you first. That doesn't mean Sammy isn't far behind in his search for you," Mitch reminded her.

Molly shuddered.

"But getting back to the subject of your secretary, I do think you'd be putting her in danger if you stayed at her condo. In fact, after we get you settled somewhere, I don't want her to know where you are."

Molly covered her face with her hands. The breakfasts she had eaten with so much pleasure now felt like a round ball of lead in her stomach.

Chapter 12

MOLLY SAID GOODBYE TO MITCH at the Omelet Shop and went to her car where she sat quietly behind the wheel. Several disturbing things had happened at breakfast.

Sammy the Grunt wants to kill her. The thought was so terrifying she slid partway down the seat and cautiously looked around. The sun-drenched main street in the small town looked peaceful. The people walking past her car in a steady stream looked friendly. Somewhere close by, Sammy the Grunt was looking for her. That thought made her mouth dry and her hands shake.

To get her mind off Sammy, she turned her thought to the other disturbing thing that had happened at breakfast. The thick protective wall she had built around her heart had been shaken. She had felt a physical shock when their eyes met. In those few seconds, she realized Mitch had the ability to awaken feelings that would once again expose her heart to a world of hurt. She couldn't let that happen.

Not again.

Picking up her cell phone, she shook her head to get Mitch out of it. Now was the time to figure out how to handle the situation with Clara. Somehow, she had to keep her safe. That meant Clara had to know what was going on, but she didn't have to know all the gory details. Not wanting to scare her, she intended to treat the situation as lightly as she could.

Clara was busy at work when she answered Molly's call. "How was breakfast with Mr. Eye...?"

"Don't say it, Clara! Don't call him that anymore," Molly pleaded. "I have trouble looking at him without laughing as it is. But you know what? Now I've decided that he looks like Ken, Barbie's boyfriend?" She paused and thought. "Come to think about it that might be even worse than Mr. Eye Candy."

"I'll bet he didn't have anything to tell you; he just lured you there with that promise."

"Oh for heaven's sake, Clara! Mitch isn't like that! He had some news to tell me, and you, too, for that matter."

"Me? How did I get mixed into this?"

"It's good news for you because I won't be your house guest anymore," Molly said, trying to sound cheerful.

"One night of sleeping with your head on my kitchen table was it, huh?" Clara joked. "But once you're home, I'll bet you won't be walking at night any more, will you?"

"I can't say that I won't. I don't walk at night because I want to, I walk because my legs won't let me do anything else," she paused to collect her thoughts. "It's like at night they have a life of their own. I hate nights! I have thought many times that I should find a night job. That would solve my problem because I'm not bothered by this problem during the day."

"Molly, you are truly weird! Maybe you *are* some form of vampire, just not a neck-biting one!"

"Enough of this vampire thing!" Molly said firmly. "Is there something that I need to take care of right now? I know there were many messages from the title and mortgage companies because I listened to them yesterday at your condo. Have you gotten back to all of them?"

"I just finished with the last one when you called. All the details for the closings at the end of the week have been taken care of. The closings will be held at the title companies."

"Thank you, Clara. You make my job easy. I don't know how I managed before you came along."

"Molly, this job saved my sanity. You know that, and I'll tell you something else," she giggled. "You can't fire me because I've made up my own filing system. You'll never figure it out, so you best keep me around!" Clara stopped her chatter when she heard a huge sigh on the other end of the line. "Molly," she asked in alarm. "What's wrong?"

Molly took a deep breath. "Clara, uh…"

"Come on, Molly! What's going on? Something you haven't told me?"

"I'm not going home, Clara," Molly said quietly. "Detective Hatch is finding a safe place for me to stay until this whole thing is over."

"Are you saying that my place isn't safe, or is there something wrong with my condo? Does the sleeping bag in the guest room have something to do with this?"

"No, no, Clara! It has nothing to do with your condo. It has something to do with your safety."

"My safety?" Clara's voice hit a high note.

"Yes, Clara, your safety. Sammy the Grunt is looking for me because he thinks I'm a witness to the two murders. I don't want him finding me at your condo because that would put you in danger, too. In fact, when Detective Hatch finds a safe place for me, you will not be told where it is."

It was Clara's turn to be out of words. "Molly, I'm so sorry this is happening to you." There was a long period of silence before Clara continued. "What are you going to do about keeping the office open? Is it safe for you to show up here?"

"Detective Hatch had no problem finding where I work, so I imagine Sammy won't have a problem either. So, no, it's not safe for me to go to the office."

Molly could hear Clara take a shaky breath. "Should I be afraid? What if Sammy shows up and thinks I know where you are?"

"Detective Hatch and I have thought of that. We've decided that the best thing is to close the office."

"But what about your business? You have closings scheduled and someone gave your name to a doctor who needs to find a house. How are you going to handle this?"

"I don't have a choice, Clara. I wish you hadn't changed your mind about becoming an agent. I sure could use you right now!" Molly couldn't see Clara, but she was sure Clara was shaking her head.

"Not on your life, Molly! The life of a real estate agent doesn't appeal to me. Half the time you work your butt off for nothing."

"Can't argue with you there, Clara, but here's what I'm asking you to do. Put the closed sign on the door and change the phone message."

"Are you going to check the phone messages, or am I?"

"You're still on the payroll, Clara, so you answer the calls from your condo. I'll keep checking in with you."

"Molly, be sure you use your cell phone when you do. If you use the landline phone at the safe place, my phone system will identify the number. I probably shouldn't know that in case this Sammy guy somehow tracks me down."

"I'm so sorry you are mixed up in this mess, Clara," Molly said sadly.

"Let's just hope this doesn't drag out indefinitely," Clara said. "Oh, before I forget to tell you, three times this morning I answered the phone and all I heard was heavy breathing. Have any idea what that's all about?"

"You mean it's not one of your secret admirers?" Molly chided her. "Yeah, I've been getting those calls at home, too. I didn't think too much of it at first, but now it's getting scary. It has to be connected with this Sammy thing, don't you think?"

"Boss, you don't pay me enough to figure out stuff like that. Is there anything else I can do for you?"

"Yes, there is something. I need you to go to my house and pack a bag for me. Do you remember where my spare house key is in the office?"

"Yes."

"Detective Hatch will meet you at my house. It wouldn't be safe for you to go there alone. He has the list of the things that I need right now."

"Okay," Clara answered. "I'll do the message thing on the phone, put the closed sign on the door, and then head for your house. Good luck, Molly!"

Clara ended the call.

MITCH'S CAR WAS NOT in the driveway when Clara arrived at Molly's house. She sat in the car, wondering if it was safe for her to go in. If it wasn't a safe place for Molly, was it a safe place for her?

Where was Mitch?

Gathering her courage, Clara got out of her car, and, while nervously looking over her shoulder, went into Molly's house.

The first thing she spotted was a big, comfortable looking chair. She pulled it around to face a window and sat down to watch for Mitch.

A pull on a handle by her right side eased the chair into a reclining position. She sighed with pleasure as her eyes closed. If Molly couldn't sleep in this chair, she really had a sleeping problem. It took only a few minutes before Clara felt herself drifting into a peaceful sleep. Abruptly she jerked herself awake and returned the chair to its upright position.

For the first time since she had entered the house, she had time to look around. Dishes on the table with dried food and an unwashed pot on the stove surprised her. An opened magazine on the sofa and a can of pop on the coffee table ruined the picture Clara had of a super-neat Molly. Her desk was always organized and tidy but her house certainly wasn't.

Clara's inspection of Molly's housekeeping skills was interrupted by Mitch's arrival. Molly had made a short list of things that she needed and Clara quickly finished the packing job.

"Is everything on the list in the bag?" he asked

"Everything I could find," Clara replied. "It's hard looking for things in someone else's house."

"Let's just hope we find the ...." Mitch stopped talking and reached for his ringing cell phone.

Clara, listening intently to Mitch's part of the conversation, couldn't make sense out of what she was hearing.

Mitch closed his phone and snorted. "This is beyond your wildest imagination, Clara," he said, and then burst out laughing. "What an ending!"

After wiping his eyes and blowing his nose, he shared the story with Clara. "It was the drug runner who was hiding in the junked car!"

"Wait a minute!" Clara cried, holding up her hands to stop Mitch. "What's with this 'runner' bit?"

"You think a big drug king-pin is going to run around distributing his poison? Not on your life! He uses others to do that, and they are called 'runners'," Mitch explained. "Now can I go on with the story?"

Clara nodded.

"The runner texted the police station that right after he had hidden the drugs in the old refrigerator, two guys showed up and stole them. That's when Sammy and his two buddies arrived. The one remaining streetlight made it possible for the guy to take two pictures with his cell phone. One is of Sammy and his two friends, and the other is a picture of Sammy killing the drug thieves!"

Clara was listening with big eyes. "Then what happened?" she asked with the intense intrigue of a little girl fascinated by a bedtime story.

"Apparently, Sammy is hiding in old man McGuire's basement. As we speak, a task force of DEA agents is on their way over there to arrest Sammy and probably his two cohorts."

"So Molly's no longer in danger? She doesn't have to hide now?" Clara asked eagerly.

Mitch was enjoying himself. "We don't know where the runner is, but I can't see where he would be a threat to her. The last line in the text message said he was turning off his phone and going into hiding. The least of his problems is jail time for delivering drugs. His biggest problem is Sammy, and he knows it."

Mitch got into his car and called Molly to tell her the good news. Just talking to her again made his heart happy.

Clara raced to the office to change the phone message and remove the closed sign from the office door.

Chapter 13

THE BASEMENT IN OLD MAN McGuire's house was musty and damp. Discarded cans and empty fast-food containers cluttered the room. The only light came from a ceiling bulb with a dangling chain.

In the dim light, Albert watched Sammy's face turn fierce as he held his cell phone to his ear. Sammy was waving his skinny arms, swearing and yelling at someone. Albert listened as Sammy shouted threats into the phone. He felt only disgust for the man. However, since Sammy had rescued him after his old gang had left him for dead, he kept those feelings to himself. Albert amused himself with the thought that no matter how angry Sammy got, one thing he couldn't do was gnash his teeth; he had nothing but black stumps left in his mouth.

Albert's eyes surveyed the assorted young boys sitting on the floor. One face stood out; it belonged to the kid Sammy had named Zeek. Albert had spotted the redheaded kid as being too intelligent to be in this bunch, and even now in the dim light, he could see that Zeek was keenly observing everything that was happening.

After ending the call, Sammy pulled Albert and Clarence aside and whispered the news that the runner never made it back to his home base, and the supplier was accusing Sammy and his men of doing away with him

"Well, did we?" asked Clarence.

"Hell, no, and that ain't all. Wait 'till you hear the rest!" Sammy's long grey hair was streaming over his face, giving him a wild look. "Before the runner shut off his cell phone and disappeared, he called his home base and reported that he had seen me and you two rushin' the guys who was stealin' the stash, and me killin' the two thieves. He's our witness!"

Albert felt Clarence poking him in the back. "We didn't do nothin'!" he whispered.

Sammy took a deep breath and continued. "And that still ain't all! The runner is the youngest son of the drug supplier!" He turned around and, with eyes squinting in the dim light, tried to make contact with the motley bunch that sat before him. "Somewhere in here," he said pointing his finger, "there's a snitch."

"Not me!" was the unanimous shout. "Not me!"

"Well, one of you is a liar, but right now I don't have time to find out who it is. Because of the snitch, the supplier knows where we're hidin'. They are headin' here, right now! So, all you kids, clear out! Go home and forget everything you've seen here!"

After the basement was empty, Sammy said, "Albert, you and Clarence come with me."

"Oh, hell," muttered Albert.

"Why ain't we gettin' out of here, too?" a nervous Clarence asked.

"Cause we have somethin' to take care of before we leave," Sammy answered as he rummaged through a pile of boxes.

"What ya lookin' for?" Clarence asked, his teeth chattering. "I'm scared! Why are we stickin' around when we should be runnin'?"

"Ah, here it is!" Sammy exclaimed as he held up a relatively sturdy wooden box.

"An empty box?" Albert asked. He was feeling as jittery as Clarence but he didn't want Sammy to know.

"It won't be empty for long," Sammy smirked as he felt behind a row of Mrs. McGuire's canned tomatoes and pulled out a large and bulging leather pouch.

Albert and Clarence watched in amazement as Sammy dumped the contents of the pouch into the box. Indeed, the box was no longer empty; it was packed with large bills and wallets full of stolen identities. "What do ya think of that, boys?" he asked smugly as he stuffed everything back into the pouch. He hesitated before he made the next decision. Finally, after taking one last look at his bloody knife, he lovingly placed it on top of the pouch and closed the box.

"Want to explain this, Sammy?" Albert asked.

Sammy grinned like a fox, his rotted black teeth making him look vicious. "This is an emergency box, my friends. We're gonna hide it, and some day, in the future, I predict it will come in handy."

"And the knife?" asked Albert.

With a smug look on his face, Sammy said, "Even if we get convicted of the murders, it's gonna drive them crazy when they can't find the murder weapon."

"But what emergency?" Clarence cried.

"Suppose all three of us go to jail over what happened here," Sammy stopped when he heard Clarence sob. "Clarence, I ain't saying we was goin' to jail, this is just in case."

Clarence looked at Albert for assurance that Sammy could be trusted. Albert avoided his eyes.

"Someday," Sammy continued, "we'll need money and identities, and the box has lots of both. But you gotta remember that we share this box. Whoever gets to it first has to leave money and identities for the other two."

Clarence, Albert, and Sammy took a blood oath that they would follow the instructions.

"Where are we gonna hide it?" Clarence asked.

"Follow me!" answered Sammy.

With the box and Mr. McGuire's shovel in hand, the three walked deep into the cherry orchard in back of the McGuire house. Sammy had been plotting this scenario for some time and knew exactly where he was going.

"You gonna bury it in here?" Clarence questioned. "How you gonna remember what cherry tree you pick? Seems to me, if you see one cherry tree, you've seen them all."

Sammy whirled around and grabbed Clarence by the collar. "Do I look dumb, Clarence?" he hissed. "You think I don't know what I'm doin'?"

Albert stopped walking, waiting to see how this confrontation would end. No one questioned Sammy and got away with it. He was so involved in the scene that he almost failed to hear sounds in the distance, which were rapidly getting closer.

"Hey, you two," he spoke quietly but distinctly. "Someone's comin'!"

Sammy and Clarence abruptly ceased their one-sided argument.

"Quick!" Sammy ordered. "Hide the box! Pick out a tree and climb it. Hurry!"

Albert and Sammy grabbed low limbs and swung up into leafy branches. Clarence, who had never climbed a tree in his life, had just managed to get his rump over a limb when a group of noisy children passed beneath them.

After the sound of chattering kids died away, Sammy swung down from the tree. "That was close!" he muttered. "Grab the box and let's get this done before someone else comes."

"Sammy," Albert bravely said, "Clarence has a point. All cherry trees do look alike, and fruit trees don't have a long life. Have you thought about that?"

"Not you, too!" Sammy griped but he didn't confront Albert. "Somewhere in here there's an oak tree; I found it the other day.

Just one. That's what we're lookin' for. Speakin' of lookin', where's Clarence?"

A garbled sound was coming from one of the trees. Albert pointed. "There he is!"

"Clarence," Sammy yelled. "This ain't no time for game playin'! Git down from that tree!"

"I can't," was the reply.

"Don't pull that crap on me! Now, git down!"

"Uh, I have a problem," mumbled Clarence.

"Nothin' like the problem we're gonna have if we don't get this box buried before the cops find us!"

"Don't yell at me, Sammy!" whimpered Clarence. "I'm caught."

Sputtering, Sammy approached the tree, looked up, and then made a strange sound that neither Clarence nor Albert had ever heard before. It was the sound of an old rusty engine trying to start on a cold winter morning; Sammy was laughing. Clarence had backed up on the limb and impaled his pants on a sharp broken branch.

Albert, seeing that Sammy was useless, climbed the tree and surveyed the problem.

"If you crawl forward far enough, it looks like the branch will pull right out of your pants," he said to Clarence.

"I've never been up in a tree before! I'm scared!"

"Little buddy, you're only five feet off the ground! Now, try what I said, because we sure don't want to be here when the cops come for us."

Gingerly, Clarence moved his body toward the end of the limb and extracted himself from the pointed branch.

"Looks like you're free!" Albert exclaimed. "So jump down and let's get outta here!"

There wasn't much of a sound when the limb broke, but Clarence made up for it when he hit the ground.

Sammy was laughing so hard he was having trouble breathing. After seeing that Clarence wasn't injured, except for having the wind knocked out of him, Albert took over. The last thing he wanted was to be in Sammy's company if the cops showed up. "Come on! Let's get this done and get out of here!" he ordered and took the lead.

Not only was there just one oak tree standing off by itself, but there was a huge rock beside it.

Sammy handed the shovel to Clarence. "Dig!" he commanded. "Somethin' bad might happen to that oak tree but nothin' is gonna happen to that huge rock. That's how we're gonna find the box when we need it."

Clarence dug a deep hole and the box was buried in short order.

The job finished, the three brushed the dirt from their hands and were heading out of town when their luck ran out. They were apprehended and arrested by a trio of black-suited Federal agents.

As they were led away in handcuffs, Clarence sobbed, Albert looked defeated, and Sammy started plotting; if there was a way to make this all go away, he'd find it.

Chapter 14

THE SUN WAS SHINING BRIGHTLY the next morning as Molly set off for work. Life was good. In fact, life was wonderful. With Sammy the Grunt removed from the picture, the threat on her life was gone. Life was back to normal. Being able to return to her neat and orderly home last night was wonderful.

Clara, her face lit up with a smile, called to Molly as she walked into the office, "Don't you just love a happy ending?"

"Good morning to you, too!" Molly greeted her secretary whose orange hair today had a slight greenish tint, "I never thought I'd be so happy just to come to work. If you remember, I'm showing a lake house today."

"Speaking of work!" Clara handed Molly a message.

Molly, message in hand, started for her office, but paused with her hand on the doorknob. "I can't believe it all resolved itself so quickly."

"Not everything, though," Clara reminded her. "The son of the supplier is still missing."

"That's right, but I can't see how he could be a threat to me. He has his own problems."

"Won't he get jail time for running drugs?"

"If they ever find him, yes."

"Wonder where he is," Clara pondered.

"Wherever he is, I'm sure the police will figure it out." Molly's forehead creased as she looked at the message in her hand. "Here's something else to figure out. Pray tell, what does this message mean?" She showed Clara a partially filled message slip.

"Oh. I was interrupted while I was writing that. You have another transferee coming in tomorrow. I didn't write his name? Oh dear. It was Dr. Somethingorother."

"Yes, good old Dr. Somethingorother!" teased Molly. "Clara, what am I going to do with you?"

"Well, he did make an appointment to see you tomorrow at ten o'clock. You can tell him you don't know his name because your dumb secretary screwed up."

DR. JAMES PARKER was not a happy man. Yesterday he had found the house of his dreams, advertised 'For Sale by Owner: Realtors welcome' in the local paper. James called the number listed under the picture and made an appointment to see the house. He had been in town for a week, but that time had been spent in meetings with his new partners. They were in the process of establishing a sleep clinic in the local hospital. Today was the first day there were no scheduled meetings, and he was free to check out the housing market.

A friend of his had given him the phone number of the Allen Real Estate office. He had left a message that he would like a ten o'clock appointment with a Miss Allen tomorrow. If he could buy this beauty of a house today, he would cancel the appointment.

The house was beyond anything he thought he could find in this small town. It was an architectural wonder made of glass and steel, set atop a rise overlooking a small lake. Annie and the kids would absolutely love it.

He knocked on the door and a man with a glass in his hand answered. Party sounds were coming from inside the house.

"Hello, I'm Dr. Parker. I have a three o'clock appointment. I assume you are the owner?"

"Yes I am, but not for long!" The man was exuberant. "A Realtor brought a buyer in to see the house, and my wife and I just signed a purchase agreement. We sold the house!"

A wave of disappointment swept over James. While he had been sitting through all those meetings, this perfect house had been out there waiting for him.

Seeing the look of disappointment on Dr. Parker's face, the seller added, "Won't you come in and have a glass of champagne with us? I tried to call you at the hotel where you said you were staying, but you weren't in your room. I'm sorry you made the trip for nothing."

James managed a smile. "I can't tell you how disappointed I am, but congratulations on selling your house."

The owner opened the door wider, and James stepped into the most beautiful house he had ever seen; soaring ceilings, skylights, and windows with a panoramic view of a serene little lake.

Standing with glasses of champagne in their hand were four people. He assumed that one was the seller's wife, and the other two had to be the lucky couple, so who was the fourth person? That one held out her hand and greeted James. "I'm Molly Allen, of Allen Real Estate. You're just about an hour late. My buyers were sure they were going to love this house so we arrived with a purchase agreement already written."

James shook her hand. "I'm James Parker, and I believe I have a ten o'clock appointment with you tomorrow morning."

"Oh, hello Dr. Parker! That's right. Imagine meeting you here!"

"Since I can't have this house, do you think you could find another one like this for me?"

Molly grinned. Life was getting even better. No one wanted her dead, and now she had a name for good old Dr. Somethingorother!

Chapter 15

CLARA, TODAY A BRASSY BLONDE with no black roots, was busy at her desk when the door opened and Molly's ten o'clock appointment walked in. Intent on checking the settlement figures on closing papers, Clara's head snapped up when she heard shuffling feet.

Standing in front of her was a very tall man. His jet-black hair was brushed straight back from a wide forehead. Eyebrows and eyelashes as dark as his hair framed a pair of amused gray eyes.

"Pardon me," he said. "I didn't mean to startle you!"

Clara's face flushed up to her tightly curled hair. "You must be Dr. Parker?"

"Yes, I am. Is Miss Allen ready for me?"

"Have a seat and I'll check."

Clara stuck her head into Molly's office but didn't see her right away. Stepping further into the room, she saw that Molly had her head down on her desk and was sound asleep. A very quiet snore bubbled from Molly's mouth. Gently, Clara shook her. "Wake up! Dr. Parker's in the waiting room."

Molly jerked awake. Looking chagrined, she shrugged apologetically at Clara.

"Have you been asleep in here for the last hour?" Clara asked. "Do you even know what you're going to show him?"

"Oh Clara! Thanks for waking me! Yes, I have houses to show him, but I fell asleep while I was waiting for a call on one. I guess they didn't call back!" She pulled herself to her feet. "How do I look?" she asked urgently. "Do I have sleep marks on my face? Should I go to the powder room and do something?"

"Wipe the drool off your chin and splash some water on your face. Do that and you'll look fine," Clara patted her on the back.

Molly's hand flew to her face. Finding a dry chin, she grinned at her secretary. "You had me going there, Clara. If you're through having fun at my expense, show Dr. Parker to the conference room and I'll meet him there."

Dr. Parker was sitting at the head of the conference table when Molly entered the room. Forgetting her fatigue, she smiled and said, "It's nice to see you again, Dr. Parker. Since yesterday I've had to live with the memory of the look on your face when you found out the house was already sold."

"It was not a happy moment! That look was sadness mixed with anger at myself," he admitted. "I've been in town all week, and if I hadn't let myself be tied up in so many meetings, I would have started my house hunting sooner."

"Are you still tied up in meetings? Do you have a schedule that we have to work around?"

"The meetings are almost over, thank heavens. I'm from out of town, but I'll be joining three local doctors in opening a sleep clinic connected with your hospital. The meetings were to arrange an agreement between the four of us and the hospital."

Molly's eyes widened. "I never heard of a clinic for sleep!"

"I was really surprised when I discovered that this part of the state is woefully behind in facilities for patients with sleep problems. There have been so many advances in this field but people around here are not getting the benefits of those findings."

Molly was listening intently to Dr. Parker. What kind of sleep problems was he talking about? Sleep walking? Snoring? Legs that won't stay still at night? She knew one thing; she wasn't going to describe what her legs did at night until after he'd bought a house from her. No one wants to buy a house from a crazy lady.

"I have chosen some houses similar to the one you lost yesterday. That house was on water. Is that a priority?"

"My kids would love living on a lake. They're not happy about leaving school and friends, but if they knew they were moving to a lake house, it might make a big difference in their attitude. Let's go for it!"

"I have one plum of a house to show you, but the listing office hasn't called back to verify the appointment. The house was built by the same builder as the one you saw yesterday. However, since the lake is a bigger, all-sports lake the price of the house is higher."

"How much higher?" he asked anxiously. "I've been to the bank and I know my mortgage limit."

Molly passed him a picture and the information on the house. Dr. Parker, when he saw the price, raised his black eyebrows and cringed.

"That's at the tip-top for what I'm qualified." But when he realized that just looking at the picture of the house made his heart beat faster, he asked hopefully, "Do you think there's any wiggle room in that price?"

"We can only try," she said smiling, recognizing a hooked buyer when she saw one. "Want to see that one first or last this morning?"

"Let's see it first. If it's anything like the one I saw yesterday, I won't have to see any more houses. Can we get into it?"

The door opened up and Clara stuck her head into the room.

"The listing office called on the Grass Lake house. The key's in the lockbox on the front door. Do you have the combination of the lock box?"

"Yes, I showed that house last week so I know the combination. Thank you, Clara."

Turning to Dr. Parker, she said, "Let's go find a house!"

Chapter 16

WITH A HUGE SMILE on her face, Molly returned to her office at noon.

"Way to go, girl!" she exclaimed to herself.

Clara, dressed in a suit of purple and pink stripes, was at her desk, looking through a catalog featuring a pleasantly plump model on the front cover. "Back early!" she said, dropping the catalog. "Run out of houses, or did you wear him out?"

"Neither! Buyers like Dr. Parker are what keep me in this business. They almost make me forget the ones like the Wise family. Well, almost," she said, as she tossed her car keys on the desk, "but not entirely."

"Which house did he like?"

"Would you believe we never got past the first one? He loved the one on Grass Lake! It was built by the same builder and similar to the beauty he missed out on yesterday."

"Are you telling me he bought the only house you showed him?" There was surprise in Clara's voice. "That would be some kind of a speed record, wouldn't it?"

"Well, you know I've sold a few I was holding open on Sunday, and that's pretty sweet."

"Well, we need a few more sweet deals to make up for all the sour ones!" Clara chuckled as she scanned the signed purchase agreement. "I see there's one contingency; his wife has to approve his choice. Do you see a problem there?"

"According to the good doctor, there won't be a problem, but she's coming to town immediately to see the house and sign off on the contingency."

"Anything else I should know before I begin my magic tricks?"

"You do magic tricks now?" Molly questioned her secretary who was trying to look mysterious.

Giving up on the look that wasn't working, Clara asked, "Why do you think all your closings never have a hitch in them?"

"No, I don't know why they never have a hitch in them, but I expect you're going to tell me."

Clara rolled her eyes. "Details, Molly. I take care of details!"

"Well, Miss Detail, I thank you. That's why you get paid the big bucks!"

Clara started to roll her eyes again.

"Clara, I saw that! Didn't your mother tell you if you do that often enough, your eyes are going to stay that way?" Molly teased. "Now, do I have any messages?"

Clara handed her a slip with a phone number written on it.

"Where's the name?" Molly asked, looking puzzled. "Any clue as to who is going to answer the phone when I dial this number?"

"I didn't write a name because I didn't know which one of his names to write. It could be either Mr. Eye Candy or Ken."

Molly stopped in her tracks. "Did he say what he was calling about?"

"Not a hint," grinned Clara, "but it didn't sound like a business call to me!"

Molly walked into her office and pulled the door closed behind her. She reached for the phone, and then her hand stopped midair. What if Mitch was calling with news she didn't want to hear? Maybe he was calling to tell her Sammy the Grunt had broken out of jail and was on his way to kill her. Selling a very expensive house this morning had given her a shot of adrenaline.

AND SO TO SLEEP

She wasn't ready to have that bubble burst so soon, but life has a way of plowing ahead.

She sighed and dialed the number.

"Detective Hatch speaking."

"Hello Mitch, Molly Allen returning your call. What's up?"

"Hey, Molly! Sounds like you recovered!"

"If no one wants to kill me, then life is good!" she responded. "But I must admit I slept with all the lights on. Oh, and can I mention that I sold a big house today?"

Mitch saw his chance. "Sounds like we need to go out and celebrate!" He held his breath.

Sounding unsure, Molly asked, "So, you're asking me out on a date?"

"I'm confused. Is there any reason why I shouldn't? Do you have a hatchet-carrying husband lurking around that I don't know about?"

"No," she laughed and then hesitated; there were things she had to tell him, and now was the time. Speaking rapidly she stated, "I haven't accepted a date for three years." She held her breath as she waited for his reaction.

There was silence on the other end. "Did I hear right?"

"I don't know." Dear God, was he going to make her repeat it? "What did you hear?" she asked.

"I heard you say you haven't dated in three years," Mitch replied.

"You heard right,"

There was more silence on the other end. "Is there a reason?"

"Yes, there's a reason," Molly said slowly, afraid he was going to ask one too many questions.

There was a long pause before he asked, "Do you ever think about dating again?"

Molly relaxed. "Sometimes," she admitted.

"Well, start thinking. Is tonight too soon?"

She hesitated for a brief second, remembering her resolve not to get involved. Since the wall around her heart had been repaired, she felt safe to say, "I'm thinking that tonight is fine."

He let out the breath he was holding. "Since I know where you live, how about if I pick you up at seven?"

"Want to tell me where we're going?"

"I'm keeping the restaurant a secret. But wear something like that red dress you had on the first time I saw you."

"That red outfit is rather dressy, so I gather you're not taking me to the Happy Burger Restaurant?"

"You got that right! See you at seven!"

He hung up, a happy man.

Chapter 17

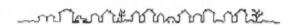

STEPPING BACK FROM her closet, Molly surveyed the mound of clothes on the bed. The search for something to wear tonight had her looking in parts of her closet she hadn't ventured into since moving day. There was still one rack in the back corner to go through.

She held up a black pantsuit she had bought for some award ceremony several years ago. It had served its purpose then, but now she shook her head. Mitch said this was some kind of celebration dinner and black was not the color for celebration. She threw the outfit on the already tall rejection pile.

Since he had remembered her red dress, maybe she should look for another bright color. One particular dress caught her eye.

There, in a bag, was the emerald green dress that she had worn only once. She had pushed it so far back into the closet she had almost, but not really, forgotten about it.

She closed her eyes and stood quietly. The raw feelings of humiliation, rejection and, yes, surprise, were just as sharp now as they were three years ago. Molly shook her head to get rid of the memory of the green dress, a memory that had a way of running through her head like a loop. Never again, she vowed, while willing more cement to fortify the wall around her heart.

She took the dress out of the dust jacket, held it up to herself, and looked into the mirror. Yes! This was what she was going to wear tonight.

Three years ago, she had worn this dress to the event that had shattered her heart and made her leery of all men.

ON THE OTHER SIDE of town, Mitch was busy. He had picked up his two nieces from day care and was trying to rush them through their macaroni and cheese dinner. Laurie and Kim sensed Mitch's eagerness for them to finish eating.

"Is something fun going to happen when we're through dinner?" eight-year-old Laurie asked.

"Why would you think that?"

"Are we going for ice cream?" Five-year-old Kim's face was bright with anticipation and her blue eyes glowed. Mitch looked at his two nieces. Ever since the girls had come to live with him, his bachelor life had changed dramatically. There was no longer time for a social life with all his new responsibilities. Having a dinner date with the nightwalker was probably a mistake. "I'm going out this evening and your Grandma Hatch is going to sit with you. What do you think of that?"

"Grandma is fun, but she keeps falling asleep! Last time she dozed off right in the middle of reading us a good story!" complained Laurie.

Mitch chuckled. "She did? What did the two of you do?"

"I just picked up the book and finished reading the story to Kim."

"Aren't you the smart one!" he said as he patted Laurie on the head. "Now finish your dinner and put the dishes in the sink. I'm going to take a shower, so, Laurie, look after your little sister. Grandma will be here in a few minutes but make sure you look through the window before you open the door."

MITCH STOOD IN FRONT of his closet, a towel wrapped around his slim waist, wondering which suit to wear tonight. The restaurant he had chosen had a strict dress code, so he knew a tie was necessary. He picked out a red silk one that looked good with his blue suit and white shirt. When fully dressed, Mitch looked into the mirror for a final check. He was surprised that his face showed nothing of the sadness that so often overwhelmed him. The grief was so thick that at times he had trouble breathing. Two years had not dulled the shock of losing his younger brother, Fred, and Fred's wife, May, in a car crash. Mitch's life had changed forever.

"Where's Grandma?" he asked as he entered the den. The girls were watching television.

"She's not here," answered Laurie, never taking her eyes off the screen.

"Did she call?" he asked. "I didn't hear the phone."

Both girls shook their heads, intent on watching their program.

Mitch was looking at his watch when the phone rang.

"Hello?"

"Mitch, it's Mom. I'm at the hospital with your dad!"

"What?" Mitch's heart skipped a beat.

"I said," she yelled into the phone, "I'm at the hospital with your dad."

"Mom, you don't need to shout! Why is Dad in the hospital?" Mitch's voice shook. "Tell me it's not serious!"

"No, it's not serious," she snickered. "He's going to be all right, but I can't leave him right now."

"Did you just laugh?" Mitch sighed with relief.

"You know him and his bike," she scoffed. "I swear he's in his second childhood!"

"Mom, get off his back about riding that bike. The exercise is good for him. So what happened?"

"Well, you know how your dad rides with his head down?" She waited until she heard Mitch grunt on the other end. "The neighbors are having some yard work done, and there was a landscaper's truck parked in the street with the ramp down in the back."

Mitch snorted. "Are you telling me that Dad rode his bike up the ramp?"

"Yep, right up the ramp into the bed of the truck. He smacked his head pretty hard."

Mitch choked on his response. "How bad is he hurt?

"He's not, but he has another dented helmet. The neighbors insisted on taking him to the hospital. Your Dad is pretty embarrassed about the whole thing and just wants to go home. When it was obvious that he wasn't hurt, the workers got a good laugh out of it."

"I guess that means you won't be sitting with the girls tonight," he said, already trying to figure out how he was going to handle the problem. "Right?"

"Goodness!" she gasped. "Look at the time!"

"Don't worry about it, Mom. I'll make other arrangements. Just stay with Dad, and I'll talk to you tomorrow. Tell Dad I'm glad he didn't break anything this time. Bye."

He looked at his watch and saw he had ten minutes to get to Molly's house. "Girls, we're going out. Grab your coats and head for the car."

"Ice cream, Uncle Mitch? Are we going for ice cream?" A happy Kim jumped off the couch to hug him.

"Well, maybe some ice cream later. Right now, we're going to see a very pretty lady. Get into the car."

MOLLY SAT IN her emerald green dress, watching for Mitch's car to pull into her driveway. It was a bit past seven, but she was determined not to be too anxious about this date. Tonight was going to be a good night, and finally, the curse would be lifted from the green dress. Only good things were going to happen when she wore it.

Mitch's car finally pulled into her driveway. She watched as he got out, opened the car's back door and helped someone out. To Molly's dismay, she saw that he was leading two small children up the porch steps. She hesitantly opened the door.

He smiled apologetically and asked, "Anyone for Happy Burgers?"

Chapter 18

WIDE-EYED, MOLLY stared at Mitch and the two girls. How could this be happening? She burst into tears and slammed the door.

The girls were shocked; Mitch could feel them shaking. He pulled them close and called, "Molly, open the door!"

"Why should I?" she sobbed.

"It's not what you think!" He was kicking himself. One phone call would have prevented this scene.

"How do you know what I think?" The sound of her blowing her nose came through the door.

"Please, Molly, talk to me!" he pleaded

"Why?" she sniveled. "So you can tell me a big lie like...like your wife doesn't understand you? I'll bet she understands you all right!"

"Come on! Don't make a scene in front of the girls. You're upsetting them!"

The door opened a crack revealing Molly's tear-stained face. She had cried so hard she had the hiccups. "I can't believe, hic, you brought your kids with you."

"Please let us in so I can explain," Mitch coaxed. "There's a reason I have them with me."

Molly looked at the scared girls who were clutching Mitch's legs.

She sighed. "Since it's apparent we aren't going to dinner, I suppose you could come in while I go upstairs and take off this, hic, dress," she conceded.

"That's a beautiful dress, Molly. I hope I have the honor of actually taking you to dinner someday when you're wearing that dress. Just not tonight."

"I'm never wearing this dress again. It's cursed! I'm giving it to Goodwill tomorrow!"

Mitch looked puzzled. "Why would you want to do that?"

"Why not?" she wailed. "Only bad things happen, hic, when I wear it!"

"Molly, believe me!" he begged. "What's happening is not a bad thing."

"You're telling me that showing up at my door with your two kids is not a, hic, bad thing?"

"If you'd just let us in, we can clear up this whole situation." He took a deep breath and then asked gently, "And I take it there's a story behind that green dress?"

With a toss of her head she replied, "Yes, but I'm not telling you!"

"Why not?"

"Well," she reconsidered, "maybe I will, but I want to hear the story behind those two girls before I, hic, share anything with you!"

With that, Molly ran up the steps and slammed the door to her room.

Kim and Laurie had stood silently while all this was going on. Laurie, being older, knew Mitch had done something very bad to the pretty lady.

"What did you do to her, Uncle Mitch?" she asked.

"I shocked her, Laurie," Mitch quietly replied. "I've handled this situation very badly."

Laurie looked up at him with tear-filled eyes. "Can you make it better?"

"I'm sure going to try."

TEN MINUTES LATER Molly came back into the room. Her hair, which she had curled for the occasion, was now hanging limply down the sides of her face. Tears had erased most of her carefully applied make-up and faded blue jeans and a sweatshirt had replaced the cursed emerald green dress.

Molly found Mitch and the girls still standing by the front door. The littlest girl was pulling on his arm, begging to leave. When Mitch bent over and whispered something that sounded to Molly like 'pizza', the little girl calmed down.

"You might as well come into the den and sit. Is this going to take long? I'm exhausted."

"Molly," he said as he gathered the girls to his side, "I want you to meet my two nieces."

"Your nieces?"

He suppressed a grin at the shocked look on her face. "Yes, I said 'my nieces'!"

"Oh."

"This is Laurie," he said pointing, "and this one is Kim. Girls, say hello to Miss Allen."

Molly felt like a deflated balloon. "Laurie and Kim, I'm very glad to meet you," she managed to say. "And, uh, I think I might have overreacted a bit."

"A bit?" Mitch's mouth twitched. "I do owe you an explanation. Something happened right at the time when I was supposed to pick you up. I suppose I should have given you a call, but the easiest thing was just to bring them with me."

Molly was trying to recover her composure. She had handled the situation badly and she knew it. Looking chagrined, she turned to Mitch. "Please forgive me for my less than hospitable

90

greeting, and girls," she hung her head and implored, "I hope you will give me a chance to redeem myself."

Mitch looked at the girls. "Think we can do that?" he asked. When the girls looked dubious, Molly reached out to them and implored, "Please?"

They looked at the pretty, redheaded lady whose eyes were red from crying and nodded their heads in agreement.

Relieved that the misunderstanding on her part had been forgiven, she sat back, surveyed her visitors, and asked, "Now, do I get to hear the story?"

"Yes," Mitch started "you see...."

"Wait a minute," exclaimed Kim, jumping up and down. "The best stories always start out 'Once upon a time.' Please start the story that way, Uncle Mitch!"

Pulling Kim into his arms, he began the story. "All right, if that would make you happy here we go. Once upon a time, I had younger brother named Fred. We were just a year apart in age, and we looked alike."

"Fred was my dad," explained Laurie.

"Yes, Laurie, Fred was your dad. After we grew up, most people had trouble telling us apart. When Fred was in fourth grade, a new girl showed up at school. Her name was May."

"That was my mom," whispered Kim as she snuggled closer to Mitch.

He paused long enough to give Kim a reassuring squeeze before continuing the story. "Fred told me he was going to marry that new girl. He never changed his mind. They were together through grade school, middle school, and right after high school, they married."

Molly was squirming. "I'm getting the feeling that this story isn't going to end, 'and they lived happily ever after'?"

"I'm afraid not." Mitch paused, sighed deeply, and then continued. "They were killed two years ago in a car accident.

May's parents were so broken up over losing their only child, they still don't have much contact with their two wonderful granddaughters." Mitch gave the girls a loving smile. "My mom and dad are in their seventies, and with no other siblings, I was the logical one to raise the girls. Insurance policies and the settlement from the accident have made life a bit easier because I can afford to hire help, but every once in a while I need Mom to fill in. She was supposed to keep the girls tonight, but Dad ended up in the emergency room and she couldn't do it."

"Oh, my!" Molly covered her face with her hands. "I'm so ashamed of myself! My concern over a spoiled dinner date and a cursed dress seems so petty compared with your story. I hope there's nothing seriously wrong with your dad."

"If I told you why he's in the hospital," Mitch's eyes crinkled, "we would have the first laugh of the evening, believe me!"

"Grandpa rode his bike up a ramp and into the bed of a truck!" laughed Laurie.

Molly raised her eyebrows.

"Dad rides his bike every day," Mitch explained. "Mom thinks he's in his second childhood, but I tell her the exercise is good for him. However, I must say he does have more than his share of accidents. He now has a replaced hip, an artificial knee, and on the shelf in the garage, he has two busted helmets...probably three now. And these are just the things I'm remembering off the top of my head." Mitch looked at Molly. "Am I forgiven for showing up for our very first date with my two nieces?"

"Yes, you're forgiven," she said, smiling. "That was quite a story."

"Now, your turn," he said eagerly. "What's this about a cursed green dress?"

"Must we go into that now?" she asked reluctantly.

"I told you my story, now the ball's in your court."

"Start the story 'Once upon a time' please," Kim pleaded.

Molly shrugged. Taking a deep breath, she looked at Mitch and gathered the courage to tell him the story that had altered her life. "Once upon a time, three years ago, I was engaged to be married to a man named Dave. He was new in town, so no one knew much about him. He was very handsome, had lots and lots of money, and he said he loved me. He sent me flowers, took me to nice places, bought me beautiful gifts, and asked me to marry him. We had a church wedding planned. He didn't have too many friends in town, but I had my family and lots of friends."

"So, where does the cursed dress come in?" Mitch asked.

"I'm getting to that. I bought a beautiful emerald green dress to wear to the rehearsal dinner. It was the perfect dress; I felt like a princess in it."

"Was that the dress you had on tonight when you opened the door?" asked Laurie.

"Yes, that's the dress," Molly said as she smiled and winked at Laurie. "A few early arrivals, mostly my family, were there when the door flew open. Several police officers rushed in, put handcuffs on Dave, and marched him out of the room!"

"Oh," gasped Kim. "That's awful! Why did they do that to Dave?"

Molly reached out and patted Kim's hand. "Well, Dave had done some bad things. He was wanted downstate by a wife, three kids, and a business partner who wanted the embezzled money back." Molly paused, "and his name wasn't Dave, either."

Mitch had listened intently to the story. "And this was three years ago?" he asked, his curiosity piqued. "Have you followed up on what happened to him?"

Molly shook her head. "At the beginning I did, but after a few months, I gave up."

"You were left to undo all the wedding plans," Mitch mused. "How did you handle that?"

Molly gave a mirthless chuckle. "Pretty much like I handled tonight.

Mitch cringed. "That bad, eh?"

"Yes, I'm afraid so."

She closed her eyes, leaned back, and continued. "For a long time after they hauled him away I was in a state of shock. The Paris honeymoon had to be called off, and all reservations had to be canceled. What a mess that was! I don't know how I would have handled it if mom hadn't stepped in and taken over."

"So you really don't know what happened then?" Mitch wasn't satisfied with Molly's reply.

"You mean to Dave? Well, I know his wife divorced him, took the house, kids, dog…she really stuck it to him. Turns out she's the sister of his ex-partner." Molly laughed when she saw Mitch's puzzled face. "I know it gets confusing, but stick with me."

"I'm sticking!"

"When Dave showed up in Detroit, he met and later married the woman who then introduced him to her brother. That's how Dave got into that partnership from which he embezzled the money. When they caught him, he still had most of the stolen funds. Those all went back to his former partner who then dropped the charges. The partner made it clear that the only reason he did that was to protect his sister and her children from further stress."

"You said, 'When Dave showed up in Detroit'. Showed up from where? Was anyone ever curious enough to look into his past?"

"Just can't help acting like a detective, can you?" Molly chuckled. "Dave had the ability to tell a good story. I'm sure he convinced all of them that he was one of the good guys. The last I heard, Dave was having trouble accepting reality and, for the short time he was in jail, he was under the observation of a psychiatrist."

"Just one more question, Molly, and then I'll quit. Did he ever say why he picked this particular area when he fled his wife and partner? Did he have any ties to people or places in this town? I'm just curious."

With a funny look on her face, Molly answered. "I'm just remembering a conversation I had with him shortly after we met. I asked him the same question and he turned on me, accusing me of being too nosy. And his face…" Molly briefly closed her eyes, remembering how shocked she had been at the malevolent expression on his face. "I really forgot all about that incident until now when you asked that question."

"I promised that was my last question about Dave, but this happened three years ago?" he asked again.

"Yes, and tonight was to be my first date since that episode." She turned to Mitch and pleaded, "Now do you see why I was so upset when you showed up with the two kids?" When Molly saw the look on Kim and Laurie's faces, she was horrified. "Girls, this has nothing to do with you; you both are adorable!"

Kim hid her face in Mitch's chest; Laurie gave Molly a mean look.

"Oh, Mitch, can you explain this to the girls? Can you make them understand that I thought I was being deceived again?" Molly was near tears.

Mitch hugged the girls. "I'm sure I can. But do you really blame your dress for all of this?"

She looked at him with narrowed green eyes. "You know something else I can blame it on?"

He grinned and said, "I say I'd blame the first incident on a bad choice and tonight was just a matter of bad timing." He paused, clapped his hands together, and asked, "Who's up for pizza?"

With all the misunderstandings behind them and after all the 'once upon a time stories' were finished, things really began to fit together. The girls adored their Uncle Mitch and were at first reluctant to share him. By the time the pizza arrived, they had allowed Molly to enter into their warm little circle.

Looking around, Mitch saw that he was the only one in formal attire. "Would anyone object if I took off my tie?" he asked.

He slipped off his tie, took off his cuff links, and rolled up his shirtsleeves.

"Now, I feel better," he announced. "But what should I do with this tie? Let's see. I could put it on Laurie."

"Why?" she asked, looking puzzled.

"To cover the pizza stain on your shirt," he teased.

"Oh!" Laurie grabbed a napkin and hastily scrubbed the front of her shirt that, indeed, had a big stain on it.

"Or," he looked around the room, "we could dress up Molly. How do you think my red tie would look on her?"

Mitch walked over to Molly. Her eyes were still red from crying, but she had a smile on her face. He approached her slowly and while looking into her eyes, placed the tie around her neck. When he brought the knot up under her chin, she held her breath. No man had been this close to her since Dave.

The bricks around her heart quivered. After three years of being very wary about any relationship involving the opposite sex, Molly was beginning to suspect that not all men were like Dave.

Chapter 19

THE HOUSE SEEMED quiet, almost deserted, after Mitch and the girls left. Molly looked at the mess left behind, and smiled at the memories. It wouldn't take her long to clean it up tomorrow when she got home from work.

The evening, if you could forget the rocky beginning, had been enjoyable. Molly held up Mitch's pizza-stained tie and remembered the warm feeling that had spread through her when he put it around her head.

Tonight, her bed did look inviting. Snuggling down into its soft warmth, pleasant memories of the evening lulled her into a deep sleep. It was midnight when the creepy-crawly demon visited one of her legs.

Refusing to wake up, Molly thrashed and kicked until the demon won. The demon always won. Sighing, she swung her legs over the edge of the bed, grabbed her robe, slid her feet into slippers, and quietly began the ritual of walking off the demon. Not turning on lights, she moved silently through the living room, heading for the kitchen.

The familiar sound of the refrigerator door opening stunned her. She froze. The light coming from its open door illuminated a strange and shadowy figure.

Startled, the intruder and Molly screamed, their voices matching in volume and intensity. The room lost its only light when the refrigerator door slammed shut.

Molly drew a thankful breath at the sound of the back door closing. The intruder was gone.

THE NOISE OF SIRENS and the invasion of spotlights had turned a quiet night in a peaceful part of town into a circus. Curious neighbors in their odd assortment of nightclothes gathered in bunches and speculated among themselves. The policemen they had watched running into the house hadn't come out. For the benefit of those who didn't know, one neighbor pointed to the owner of the house. Some of them recognized the small redheaded person as the woman who walked at night.

Mitch pulled Molly away from the crowd. When he put his arms around her and she didn't protest, he buried his face in her hair and pulled her close. The murmur from the spectators grew louder when a police officer came out of the house and approached them. Reluctantly, Mitch dropped his arms and stepped away from Molly. "Find anything?" he asked.

The police officer shook his head, "No, nothing has been disturbed and Miss Allen has already said nothing seems to be missing."

"But how did he get in my house? I'm sure all the doors were locked." Molly didn't think she needed to tell them about her little quirks. Checking the locked doors several times before bed was one of them.

One by one, the neighbors shuffled back to their homes, heading for beds that were no longer warm. The police left after another search of the house.

Mitch turned to Molly. "Would you mind if I go back into the house with you? I'd feel better if I looked around. Maybe they missed something."

"I don't know if I'll ever feel safe in that house again. But please do come in with me," she said as she led him into the house.

Inside, Molly watched Mitch as he scaled the steps, two at a time, and disappeared into an upstairs bedroom. She shuddered. Her privacy had been invaded and a feeling of revulsion swept over her. Crying softly, she failed to hear footsteps sneaking up behind her. Suddenly, she found herself being pulled tightly against someone whose hand was smashing her mouth.

Struggling violently, she almost failed to hear the frantic whisper, "No, no, you gotta listen! Please! You gotta listen!"

The attacker waited until she was motionless. "I'm going to remove my hand, but please, please don't scream," the voice whispered. "Understand?"

Molly, unable to make a sound, nodded her head. When the hand was removed, she turned around and faced her attacker. Before her stood a boy who was looking at her with pleading brown eyes. To her horror, he burst into tears and threw his arms around her neck.

AFTER CHECKING THE UPSTAIRS, Mitch returned to the living room where he had left Molly. "If there's something to be seen, I sure didn't see...." He stopped.

Molly was standing in the middle of the room locked in a tight embrace with a tall, adolescent boy whose sobs were mingling with her comforting murmurs. She caught Mitch's eye and managed to shrug her shoulders, telling him he wasn't the only one who didn't know what was going on.

The boy's sobs quieted. He untangled himself from Molly and held out his two hands. "Go ahead and handcuff me," he said quietly. "I'm ready to turn myself in."

Mitch scratched his head. "I guess it would help if we knew who you are."

"My dad's the guy with all the drugs," the boy said his face scrunching up, "and he's going to kill me!" he sobbed.

"Now, now," soothed Molly.

"Settle down, young man," Mitch said kindly. "And I take it you were the one Miss Allen saw in her kitchen?"

The boy wouldn't meet their eyes.

"Tell us why you think your dad is going to kill you," Mitch spoke gently.

"I did something he told me I couldn't do," he sobbed.

"What's your name, son?" Mitch asked.

"Mike," the boy said, swiping his sleeve over his nose. "It's really Michael, but everyone calls me Mike."

Not wanting to send the boy into another crying fit, Mitch asked gently, "So Mike, do you want to tell us what you did that is so bad?"

"I was supposed to stay away from my dad's business," Mike's sad brown eyes were full of fresh tears. "I'd been begging him to let me be the one to put the drugs in McGuire's junky old refrigerator. I was the one who came up with the idea of hiding them there, but he told me I couldn't do it."

Mitch and Molly's eyes locked; this boy was the missing drug runner.

Mike sat quietly with his head down. The tears had left tracks that were streaking his dirty face. "I talked the regular runner into letting me make that drop. I knew it was wrong, but the refrigerator thing was my idea."

"Just that one time?" asked Mitch.

"No, for several drops. That's how I happened to see the walking lady and one night I followed her to see where she lived. When I heard Sammy tell two of his guys that they had to get rid of the walker," he turned to Molly, "I knew they were talking about you and since we were both in danger, I figured I should warn you. But I never had the chance to do it."

Molly was curious. "And where have you been living"

"In your attic, Ma'am."

Mitch raised his eyebrows and looked at Molly. "Did you know you had an attic?"

Molly was dumfounded. "My attic? I don't think you can call that small space under the roof an attic. I don't even know how you'd get into it!"

The kid grinned, his braces flashed, and then he shuddered. "I took the cover off a vent in the roof and crawled in. Lots of spiders!"

"The roof?" Molly cried. "How in the world did you get up on my roof?"

"Ma'am, that big old tree in the back made it easy."

Molly was sputtering. "I..I can see how you got into the crawl space from the roof, but how did you get into my house from there?"

Mike looked puzzled. "You don't know about the opening in the ceiling? It's your house."

"Yes, it's my house, but I don't know about an opening in a ceiling. Where is it?"

"Want me to show you?" Mike asked.

"For right now, just tell me."

"In the closet ceiling of the spare bedroom," answered Mike. "There's a pull-down ladder, too."

Molly sat quietly, thinking about all the time she had lived with someone hiding in an attic that she didn't even know she had.

Along with getting her doorbell fixed, she would hire someone to nail that ceiling access door shut.

"So," Mitch said to the boy, "you're the one who witnessed the murders, hid under the car and took the pictures?"

"Yes," the kid replied. "I wanted pictures to show my dad for a couple of reasons. When he arranges for drugs to be dropped, he expects instant money in payment. When he doesn't get it...." Mike shuddered. "I hate violence. The other reason had to do with Sammy; my dad is no friend of Sammy the Grunt! That picture of him killing the two guys would come in handy if he ever tries to double-cross dad again." After a pause, he asked, "Was that a bad thing to do?"

"I don't know very many grown men who have the guts and the knowledge to do what you did. Most of the guys in my department don't know how to turn on the computer let alone send pictures from a cell phone. It was a very good thing that you did, son. But how did you know where to send them?"

Mike held up the newest and most expensive cell phone that drug money could buy. "This phone is loaded! Any information I need, it's all here," he boasted, "the Internet and even GPS!"

Molly raised her eyebrows and silently mouthed to Mitch, "GPS?"

Mitch shrugged.

Mike giggled. "Wanna hear something funny?" he asked. When no one said anything, he went on. "One of the two guys with Sammy is not too bright. I think they called him Clarence. Anyhow, I knew that if I took a picture, there would be a flash and a click."

"You're right," exclaimed Mitch. "How did you get away with it?"

"I took one of the pictures when two of the guys were looking at each other. The only one who would see it was Clarence and I figured no one would put much stock in anything he said. The other picture, the one where Sammy was killing the two guys...," Mike swallowed hard and shook his head. "That was awful! I don't think I'll ever forget that." He shivered and then continued. "I figured they were so busy fighting they wouldn't notice a flash. But I did hold my breath because I knew what Sammy would do to me if he saw me."

"Oh, my!" exclaimed Molly. "That was a dangerous thing to do, Mike."

"Clarence told Sammy he saw a firefly!" laughed Mike.

"What did Sammy do?" Molly asked, getting into the story.

"He grabbed Clarence, called him a mama's boy, and told him to grow up. Man, was I relieved!"

Mitch looked at the boy with new eyes. "Son," he said, "It was a foolish but brave thing to do. And, you're right. Had Sammy seen that flash...!"

Mike cringed, remembering the moment. "I know I'm in trouble for running drugs, and I accept that," he said seriously. "But it's Sammy I'm scared of. My dad has told me stories about him."

"Well, I guess the news didn't make it up to the attic, but Sammy and his two men have been arrested," said Mitch. "Sammy's not going to kill anybody."

Mike's whole body jerked. "What? You mean I turned myself in for nothing?" His eyes were wild. "Shi...crap!"

The boy looked at Molly. "Sorry," he mumbled. "I turned myself in because I figured that was the only way I'd be safe from Sammy. Shi...oot! Now I'm in trouble, and my Dad's in trouble, too, isn't he?" He burst into tears again.

Mitch and Molly exchanged glances. "How old are you, Mike?" Mitch asked.

"Fifteen," sobbed the boy.

"Think the court will treat him as a juvenile?" Molly asked.

"I can't say, because it depends on the judge," Mitch replied, "but running drugs is a pretty big offense."

When Mitch called his office for backup, the dispatcher commented on the howling in the background. "You torturing someone, Detective?" she asked.

"No," answered a grim-sounding Mitch. "That's the sound of a very unhappy boy."

After Mitch finished his call, the room was quiet except for a sob or two. Finally, Mike said, "You wanna know why I was looking in your refrigerator?"

"Looking for something to eat?" Molly guessed.

Mike nodded. "I've eaten some of your food, and I'll pay you back, honest." He crossed his heart. "I made a mess in the kitchen the day a woman came in and packed stuff in a bag. I was afraid she was gonna tease you about it." He paused for a moment, and then said to Molly, "You really don't have anything good to eat in your refrigerator."

Molly's head jerked up. "You hide in my attic, mess up my kitchen, eat my food, sneak around my house and scare me to death, and now you have something to complain about?"

Mitch was trying to hide his grin behind his hand. "Mike, just what did you find in her refrigerator?"

"Uh, mustard, a bottle of catsup, a jar of olives, and a quart of milk. I did drink some of the milk," he admitted. "But I replaced it with water."

Molly made a face. No wonder her cereal had tasted funny that morning.

"Why are we talking about food," she asked him.

"Because I'm hungry!" Mike exclaimed.

Mitch grinned. "Think you could make him a mustard, ketchup, and olive sandwich?"

"No, because I'm out of bread. Tell you what, Mike," she called back as she headed for the kitchen, "I'll make you a bowl of cereal with the watered-down milk and see how you like it!"

IT WAS A SILENT HOUSE AFTER Mike was taken away. Mitch had asked them not to put handcuffs on the kid, and they hadn't.

"Want me to stay with you for a while?" he asked Molly, hoping she would agree.

Molly was silent as she considered the offer. Part of her wanted to say yes, but her fear of being entangled in a relationship was still strong.

"No, I think I can handle it." She turned to him and managed a smile. "I'm so relieved that all this is really over. Just knowing Sammy and his men are in jail and not plotting to kill me is a wonderful feeling! The knot in the pit of my stomach is almost gone."

"Almost?" asked Mitch.

"I guess I shouldn't, but I feel bad for Mike."

"I'll put in a good word for him. After all, he single-handedly solved the murders. Molly, I'll ask you again; do you want me to stay around for a while tonight?"

"Thank you, but no," she said as she led him to the door. "I want to tell you that I really enjoyed the first part of this evening. Your nieces are darling! And thank you for forgiving me for over-reacting."

With regret, he walked out the door.

Once she was alone, Molly didn't feel so secure. Another silent phone call puzzled her. Now that she was no longer a suspected witness, shouldn't the calls stop?

Dressed in her nightgown, she grabbed a blanket, walked out of the bedroom and settled on the recliner. Her sleep was peaceful until the burning demon visited.

Throwing off the blanket, she headed for her computer. She found that getting her mind off her legs could bring some peace, so she started to write a story. The characters made her chuckle and sometimes they did things that surprised her.

She pulled up the Document section, clicked on 'Untitled' and read the beginning of the story she had started several nights ago. She grinned to herself; this story had possibilities! She reread Chapter One, typed 'Chapter Two' and, with fingers poised above the keyboard, waited for inspiration to kick in. Twenty minutes later, she admitted defeat; she deleted Chapter One and shut down the computer.

Resigned, she walked from room to room until dawn was peeking through the window. When the alarm went off, she woke where sleep had finally beaten the demon. She was stretched out on the living room floor.

Chapter 20

AN EXHAUSTED MOLLY put on a pleasant smile and headed for Grass Lake to meet the Parker family. With the events of last night fresh in her mind, she wondered how she was going to get through the day.

Today, Mrs. Parker was to approve or reject the house her husband had chosen. The weather had cooperated. Sun shining on the lake's clear spring water reflected back the blue of the sky.

Both Molly and Dr. Parker held their breath as his wife and their two children inspected the house for the first time. Dr. Parker sighed with relief when his wife exclaimed, "I love it!"

The parents, expecting to find their children upstairs fighting over who got the bigger bedroom, were surprised to hear laughter coming from outside. Molly looked out the window. "Dr. Parker!" she exclaimed. "Did you see that? Your daughter just got pushed off the dock!"

"Relax," he grinned. "She won't be in the water for long. Those two kids swim like fish. We have a swimming pool in our back yard and they live in it all summer."

"I'm glad they're riding back to town in your car and not in mine," Molly chuckled.

"Looks like you've sold us a house, Miss Allen, and I don't feel bad about losing that other house. I like this one better."

"I love it when things work out. By the way, did you get the sleep clinic problems all settled?"

"I'm glad you mentioned the clinic, because I'll be sending you an invitation to our open house."

"Why, thank you, Dr. Parker!" she said as they walked toward her car. "I must admit that the idea of a clinic for sleep has made me a bit curious. I can't imagine what you would do at a sleep clinic!"

He opened the car door for her. "Come to the open house and find out!"

"I'm looking forward to it." Before she pulled away, she wound down the window, waved and smiled. "Don't forget to send me an invitation!"

BROWN-HAIRED CLARA was filing her purple-glazed nails when Molly returned to the office.

"Girlfriend, about time you came to work! I've been sitting here with nothing to do and no one to talk to," Clara complained. "Nothing exciting ever happens to me."

Molly perched on the edge of Clara's desk. "You want to hear about excitement?" she asked, leaning over to look Clara in the eye. "You want to hear about an intruder living in an attic you didn't even know you had?" Molly couldn't help but grin at the shocked look on Clara's face.

When Molly finished the account of last night's adventure, Clara exclaimed, "When I say I want excitement, I'm talking about having a good-lookin' guy wink at me. You can keep your idea of adventure. I don't think my heart could stand it!"

No one spoke for a few moments. With the McGuire's Alley murders behind them, it was life as usual. Clara broke the silence with a complaint. Waving the file in the air, she said to Molly, "You need to sell more houses to keep me busy or I'll soon have no fingernails left to file!"

"Well, here's something you can do." Molly handed her the signed contingency removal from the purchase agreement. "Another detail down the drain! Mrs. Parker loved the house, so full speed ahead toward the closing on this deal. Do we have a closing date?"

"Yes," Clara replied. "The mortgage has been approved, and the title company is working on the closing papers as we speak. They think the end of this week should finish it up."

"Good work, Miss Detail! You earn your big bucks every day!"

Clara smirked. "Will I get bigger bucks if I give you your messages?"

"I don't know about bigger bucks, but you just might get fired if you don't!" Molly threatened with a chuckle in her voice.

Clara nodded at the stack of messages. "The one on top is the most important."

Molly looked at the top message. Mitch had called. He answered on the second ring.

"Mitch, it's Molly."

"Oh, hi!" He sounded pleased. "I was hoping it was you!"

"I just got back into the office."

"After last night, I'm surprised you even went to work today," he remarked quietly.

"I find that going to work is easier than staying in that house," she confessed.

Mitch was quiet. "Maybe we should just think about the first part of the evening and not dwell on what happened later." He was fumbling for words. When Molly didn't reply, he confessed, "I really liked the first part, and I was intrigued with the green dress story."

She sniffed. "The memory of the green dress plays like a loop constantly running in my mind."

"Well, we'll just have to work on new and better memories for you, Molly. Think we could do that?" he asked.

"I'm really not in the market for new memories, Mitch. Since that incident, I've never allowed myself to be in a position to be humiliated like that again."

"Is that why you haven't dated in three years? You don't trust your judgment?"

"And why should I trust my judgment? I ask you, Detective Hatch, why should I?"

He took his time before replying. "Because if you never take any chances, what fun is there in life?"

"Ha! I'll take a routine, uneventful life over a tumultuous one any old day," she replied with feeling.

"So our dinner date wasn't threatening to you?" He chuckled before he added, "The dinner that we never had?"

"My better judgment had momentarily left me because you said it was just a celebration. I admit I was excited enough to dress up in my cursed green dress, but that's history now. I've recovered my better judgment." Eager to change the subject, Molly said, "Mitch, I want to tell you again how much I enjoyed the first part of last night. Your two nieces are darling."

"They liked you, too," he replied, glad to be talking about something else. "Sometimes it's hard for them to share me because they think I'm going to disappear the way their parents did."

"You can't blame them for feeling like that. By the way, how's your dad?"

"Mom brought him home from the hospital right after the doctors figured nothing was hurt but his pride," Mitch said.

"He's lucky!"

"Lucky, but embarrassed. His bike-riding buddies are teasing him unmercifully!"

"Back to the reason I'm late getting into the office. Remember I told you I had just sold a big house on a lake? I think it was one of the things we were going to celebrate at dinner last night."

"I remember," Mitch replied.

"The sale was contingent upon his wife's approval. She and their two kids flew into town just to see the house," she explained.

"Did she like it?"

"Fortunately, she did, and so did the kids."

As Mitch began to lead the conversation toward setting another date, he felt like a teenager; his mouth was dry and his face was flushed. He stammered, "Uh, would you consider it a date if I offered to cook a celebration dinner tomorrow tonight? Nothing special, just spaghetti. If we call it a celebration dinner and not a date, would that make you feel better?" He held his breath.

"How can I say yes when I just told you I had gotten back my better judgment?" she wailed.

"There are a couple of reasons I can think of just off the top of my head. One is my red tie."

"What about your red tie?"

"I want it back," he said flatly. "That's my favorite tie."

"Uh," she hesitated, not knowing quite how to say it, "Uh, would you like it before or after I have it cleaned?"

"Cleaned? Why does it need to be cleaned? It was spotless when I took it off last night!"

"It might have been spotless before you put it around my neck," she replied.

"Are you telling me you got pizza stains on it?"

"You might say that."

"You and Laurie! You both need bibs! But back to the subject of tomorrow night. I make a mean pot of spaghetti, and no one has died from it...that I know of. I keep my evenings free for the kids; guilty feelings, I suppose. I try to be with them as much as I can in the evenings. You tell me where you want me to pick you up, and the girls and I will be there at five."

Molly hesitated. She could handle this. "Pick me up at home. Can I bring anything? A salad? Dessert?"

He had been holding his breath. "Just your lovely self and my red tie."

Chapter 21

MOLLY SAILED THROUGH the morning with a feeling in her heart that she hadn't felt in a very long time. Agreeing to have dinner with Mitch and the girls must have been the right decision because all of a sudden, life was good and life was fun! No problem seemed too big, and no little detail irritated her. She was humming to herself when Clara popped her red head into the room.

"Did you read all the messages I gave you, or just the one from Mitch?" Clara teased.

Molly sighed. She didn't feel like going back to work. "Oh, that's right. There were more, and no, I haven't looked at them. Any one in particular I should start with?"

"Yes, look at the one with the name Henry Baker on it."

"I see it. Clara, your handwriting is so bad I can't read it. What does Henry Baker want?"

"He wants you to show him the old farm house on Miller Road."

"Well, I certainly can make an appointment and show him the property but it's not my listing. Did he say why he called me and not the lister of that property?"

"He mumbled about someone giving him your name. Said he was told you are a good agent and easy to work with."

"Flattery works! I'll take compliments anywhere I can get them. When does he want to see it?"

"Sometime next week. He said he'd call and make an appointment when he was sure of the day."

"That old farm has been on the market for years," said Molly. "I can't imagine what shape the house must be in by now."

"You mean no one lives there?"

"Not for years. There was some kind of tragedy connected with that house. The property is quite large. I'll have to look up specifics before I show it, but it's a lot of acreage. Maybe Henry Baker is a developer. Clara, is there another message I should look at?"

"How about the one from your old buyer, Mr. Wise."

"I thought the Wises were gone forever," Molly mused.

"I think most of them are; only one Wise is left. He wants you to find him a small apartment."

"Oh dear!" Molly said as she looked at the message. "I had the feeling there were some bad things going on in that marriage. Sometimes a transfer shakes up the relationship and old hurts and bad feelings surface. Did he say anything I should know about?"

Clara paused to think. "No, just that he would like to meet with you this afternoon to find a small apartment quickly. He wanted me to be sure to tell you that he's not in a position to buy anything right now, so he's looking for a rental."

"Poor guy!"

After talking to Mr. Wise on the phone, she drove to his hotel and found him standing outside waiting for her. He looked different. When she had first met him and his family, he appeared to be the commander of his own little army. The man waiting to be picked up had obviously lost the war.

"Good to see you again, Mr. Wise!"

"Good morning, Miss Allen! I don't have a car, so thanks for picking me up. I need to talk to you about my changed circumstances because I have to rent and not buy; at least, not now."

"Clara told me that already, Mr. Wise. We're going back to my office to look at what's available and then see if we can get into any of them this afternoon."

The afternoon found Mr. Wise and Molly touring though seven apartments. Although some were better than others, Mr. Wise wasn't pleased with even the best ones.

"Will there be more apartments to see tomorrow?" he asked hopefully.

"I won't know until I see the new listings tomorrow morning. Can I reach you at your hotel if I find anything new to show you?"

"I'll be at work. I start the new job tomorrow morning," he said. "I'll call you from work and share my new work number with you."

"I'll wait for your call, then."

"Miss Allen, can I ask another favor?" he raised his eyebrows and smiled at her.

"I guess so. What?"

"Could you please drop me off at the car rental office? I need to get a set of wheels so I can drive to work tomorrow."

"Be happy to!"

Molly didn't go back to the office after leaving Mr. Wise. Clara assured her over the phone that, she, Miss Detail, could handle everything. Molly stopped at the store for milk and cereal for tomorrow's breakfast, and then headed home.

Home seemed quiet when she unlocked the door and walked in. Last night had been so hectic. Her thoughts were on Mike who was in jail waiting for a decision on how he would be tried. The pizza party seemed so long ago, but the evidence was still there because she hadn't bothered to clean up after Mitch and the girls had gone.

In the middle of smeared paper plates and napkins lay Mitch's red tie. Molly smiled. She didn't intend to give that tie back to him. She imagined the red tie fighting and defeating the curse on her emerald green dress. Maybe she wouldn't give that dress to Goodwill after all. Maybe she would save it for some very special occasion. The thought of such an event made her dream of possibilities she hadn't considered for the past three years.

Reluctantly, she cleaned up the living room, threw away the leftover pizza, and took the box to the trash. All traces of the little party were gone, but not the memory of the warm feeling. Being part of a family, even for that short period, had awakened emotions she thought were dead. Mitch and the two girls had accepted her into their close little group.

After Dave, Molly had given up all hope of finding someone she could trust again. She had trusted Dave with all her heart. With him, she thought she had a future full of love, children, and a home. He had even promised her a dog. Three years ago, having children was a very good possibility. Now at thirty-five, Molly wondered if Dave had also taken away that possibility.

Could Mitch be different? He certainly seemed to be successfully shouldering the responsibility for his dead brother's girls. How many men did she know who would even consider taking on such a task? He wasn't an embezzler or a dead-beat husband because, to become a police officer, his past had been investigated. Too bad no one had screened Dave's past before he'd swept her off her feet.

She put a frozen dinner into the microwave and set the timer. It had been a busy day and she hadn't gotten very much sleep last night.

Damn legs!

Cleaning up after dinner wasn't much of a task. Frozen dinners aren't that satisfying, but then cooking for one person isn't that satisfying, either. She smiled when she thought about dinner tomorrow night. It was fun to think about Mitch cooking for them.

She dreaded the prospect of the long evening ahead of her. Nothing on television appealed to her. A mystery movie finally caught her attention, but half way through it, her legs began their nightly song. "Walk me, walk me, walk me!" Sighing, she stood and stepped back and forth in place while she watched the movie to its end.

When the eleven o'clock news came on, she watched it while walking around the living room. With each lap, she caught her reflection in a wall mirror. What she saw was a small and tired-looking redheaded woman with eyes that drooped from lack of sleep.

Tonight, she feared, was going to be a repeat of most of her nights, except now she was afraid to venture outside for a walk around the block. The bad guys were all in jail, but the double homicide in McGuire's Alley had changed the way she thought about her neighborhood.

Grabbing her pillow and blanket, she settled down on the recliner chair. It didn't take long for the leg demon to appear. "Walk me, walk me, walk me!"

Instead, she sat down at her computer and worked on a new story until one of her characters got himself into a complex situation and she had no idea how to write him out of it.

The digital clock showed 3:00 A.M. when Molly gave in, turned off her computer and crawled into bed. By three-thirty, sobbing in frustration, she was sitting up with her offending legs swinging over the edge.

This night was just a repeat of many others.

Chapter 22

MORNING FOUND MOLLY stiff and sore. It was almost dawn when she had finally stretched out on the living room floor and fell asleep.

As she painfully pulled herself to her feet, she could hear the alarm going off in her bedroom.

It was strange that legs that had plagued her all night were now nice and calm. How easy it would be to crawl into that inviting bed and sleep. A long hot shower limbered up her aching body and a cup of strong coffee made her world livable again.

Molly reveled in the beauty of the area as she drove to work. The sun was shining brightly and the water on the lake was sparkling indifferent shades of blue.

"Another beautiful day in paradise!" she called to Clara as she entered the office. "Any new apartments on the market today?"

Clara was in the process of starting a pot of coffee. Molly could see a plate of cookies on Clara's desk.

"Good morning to you, too!" Clara called back. "Have a cookie. I made them from an old family recipe."

"Sure you did," teased Molly as she bit into one. "I'll bet money the old family recipe was on the back of the chocolate chip package."

Clara laughed. "You got me there! Look at your messages. Mr. Wise left you his new work number and he wants to know if you have anything to show him, and Henry Baker wants you to meet him at the farm house on Miller Road."

"Wait a minute!" Molly yelled, waving a half-eaten cookie at her secretary. "Since when do I meet new buyers at vacant houses? Lord, he could be Jack the Ripper for all we know!"

Clara was shaking her head. "No, no, no!"

"And what makes you so sure, Missy?" Molly challenged.

"Because he gave me references, and I've checked them. He's a very well established developer downstate, and all of them had nothing but praise for the properties that Henry Baker develops. So there!"

"When is this going to happen?"

"Tomorrow at three o'clock."

"Okay, but I'll have to do some research on that property because I really don't know much about it. I still don't understand why he didn't call the agent who listed it. But that's tomorrow. Today I have to find something for Mr. Wise."

Indeed, more apartments had come on the market. After picking up Mr. Wise at his new place of business, she drove him to see every one of them. None was acceptable.

They walked out of the last apartment around noon. "Could I buy you lunch before you take me back to work?" he asked.

Since there was nothing urgent on her afternoon's schedule, Molly accepted. She picked out a small family restaurant that she knew had good food. It wasn't until almost the end of the lunch when Mr. Wise started talking about his home situation.

"I've been wanting to apologize to you," he started.

"To me? For what?" Molly looked surprised.

"I'm still shaking my head over the things that happened the day you showed us houses," he said quietly.

"You mean besides Toby getting his head stuck?" Molly grinned. "I thought I had gone through about everything possible in the real estate business, but he proved me wrong!"

"No," he smiled. "When I look back on that day, Toby's getting his head stuck was the least of it. He'll never do that again!"

"So what things are you talking about?" she asked, looking puzzled.

"I guess I was embarrassed by my wife's actions and attitude that day. You didn't deserve that kind of treatment."

Molly shrugged. "I chose this profession. Things happen."

Mr. Wise continued. "And there's something else going on. For some time now, things haven't been good between my wife and me. She tried to talk to me, but I pretended nothing was wrong. She got upset every time I mentioned the transfer. I figured she would eventually come to grips with it and accept it. But she isn't accepting it and I'm sure you figured that out." He shook his head and kept his eyes on his plate.

They sat quietly for a minute.

"Well, let's get you back to work," Molly said, changing the subject. "How much time is your new employer giving you to find an apartment?"

"They'll let me look as long as it's a reasonable time. I really appreciate your help, Miss Allen."

Before Molly could leave, Mr. Wise, his face red, asked, "Uh, Miss Allen, would you, uh, consider going with me to dinner and a show one of these nights?"

Molly's mouth dropped open. Mr. Wise, a married man, was asking her out on a date? "It's kind of you to ask, Mr. Wise, but I have a rule never to date my customers," she managed to answered. She wanted to include 'married men' in that statement, but she kept her mouth shut.

Embarrassed, he lowered his head and walked away.

AFTER LEAVING MR. WISE, Molly had the strongest urge to go on home. She would love to be able to crawl into her bed and sleep for a few hours. However, business always comes first, so she reached for her phone.

When the phone rang on Clara's desk, she put down her nail file and answered, "Allen Real Estate! May I help you?"

"Hi, Clara, it's Molly. You certainly can help me; tell me there's nothing going on at the office so I can just go home. I'm exhausted!"

"You had another one of those nights?" Clara asked sympathetically.

Molly snorted. "Are there any other kind?"

"I'm going to Google 'Vampires'," Clara declared.

"I'm not a vampire!" Molly cried. "I just have legs that feel like they've been plugged into the wall socket...but only at night."

"Ha, see there? Vampires only bite at night. Your legs do funny things only at night. My idea is not as farfetched as you might think. Laugh if you must, you won't hurt my feelings, but back to your question about wanting to go home...sorry about this. Judy from White Realty showed your listing on Elizabeth Street."

"That's great! I've done a lot of advertising on that property. Did her buyer like the house?"

"That's the problem. When they opened the door, the buyer swore she smelled gas and wouldn't go any further into the house. Since it's your listing, Judy called here to tell you about it."

"Oh, shoot. The sellers are out of town this week so that means I have to take care of the problem myself. Thanks, Clara. They say 'No rest for the weary', and I sure am weary." Molly hung up and called the gas company.

The man listened to Molly's problem and then instructed her to wait at the house for the service men from the gas company to show up. "Sit in your car and wait for us. Do not, I repeat, do not go into the house."

Molly obediently sat in her car in front of her Elizabeth Street listing and waited. She realized that looking at her watch didn't make the time pass any faster, but that didn't stop her from looking. It was taking forever for someone to show up. She leaned her head against the window of her car and fell asleep.

A service man pounded on the window and, when Molly opened her eyes, made a motion for her to roll down the window.

"Sorry to wake you, Miss, but are you the one with the house key?"

Taking the keys, the man and several more men from the company went into the house.

Molly's neck was stiff. A look at her watch told her she had been asleep for an hour. They had made her wait a whole hour before they showed up, and now she had to wait while they tried to find the gas leak.

Forty-five minutes later, the door of the house opened and the men filed out. The man returning the key said, "Whoever smelled gas in that house has a nose like a bloodhound! Even our gas detector had trouble finding the leak because it was so small; but there was a leak and we fixed it."

Mitch and the girls were picking her up at five o'clock and it was already three-thirty. Molly called the office and told Clara she was going home now, and if the office was quiet, she could go home, too.

BY A QUARTER TO FIVE, Molly was ready. Finding something to wear this time wasn't as hard as it was the first night when she thought they were going to a fancy restaurant; tonight was casual. She chose a matching skirt and sweater the color of melted yellow lemon sherbet. A search through her drawers produced a headband of a darker yellow. She swept her red hair back off her face and held it in place with the headband. She looked tired, but a touch of pink on her cheeks and lips brought life to her face. Her green eyes grinned back at her. "Not bad, old girl, I must say, not bad!" she muttered to the image in the mirror.

With fifteen minutes left to wait, she thought of a problem. The doorbell hadn't worked when she had moved into the house and not all her good intentions to get it fixed helped right now with Mitch and the girls on their way. Molly decided she would pull the big chair to the window and watch for them.

The one piece of furniture Dave had brought to their union was the recliner she had been sleeping on the past few nights. He enjoyed sitting in it while he watched his never-ending sports shows. The big chair would claim him after a few innings or quarters, and Dave would soon be dead to the world.

She sank into the soft chair, put it into the recline position and promptly fell asleep.

Chapter 23

MITCH WAS HAVING TROUBLE concentrating on Captain Hilburn's morning briefing. He was picturing Molly's face when she opened the door and saw him with his two nieces. What a blunder on his part.

Mitch's mind was busy replaying the scene. He mentally kicked himself for not calling Molly and explained his situation before he arrived at her door. Not paying attention, it was a change in the captain's voice that brought him back to the briefing.

"All recently promoted personnel will be sent to the Upper Peninsula for a week of intensive training!"

He looked around the room for others who had surprised looks on their faces. He saw a redheaded man across the room abruptly sit up straight and raise his eyebrows. "He must be another new one," he muttered to himself. "Dang, he looks familiar!"

The Captain continued. "Sorry about the short notice, but there's been a scheduling conflict with another precinct. The next two weeks are the only available times for our training. You have two choices: you can go this week or you can go next week. Pick one. Please report to my office after this briefing and tell me your preference."

The Captain's message raised a soft groan from his men.

"Again," he repeated, "let me say I'm sorry about the short notice."

No way was Mitch going away this week. Breaking a dinner date with Molly and not having time to explain what was going on was just not going to happen. By going the next week, he would have time to arrange the girls' schedule so that they could spend time with May's parents.

Her parents had been patient and understanding about the care of their daughter's children. The death of their only child had brought them grief that was almost too much for them to handle, and they were more than happy for Fred's brother to take on the responsibility. However, lately, they had shown interest in getting to know their granddaughters better. A week's visit while he was in training would be perfect. Mitch decided that he wouldn't tell the girls about the visit until after tonight's dinner. He wanted them on their best behavior.

He made two calls. One to May's parents, and the other to report his choice of classes to the Captain's office. The Westins were delighted. After two years of adjustment, they were ready to move on. They needed to get acquainted with May's daughters. A week's visit would be a good start.

The rest of the day passed in a haze of making a grocery list and overseeing his name being stenciled on the office door. He was relieved when he was able to slip out of the building without being questioned.

On the way home, he stopped at the grocery store to pick up salad greens and crusty garlic bread to go with the sauce he had already made. His last stop was at the daycare center to pick up the girls.

"All right, girls. You all know what your jobs are. Clean up your rooms, pick up your toys, wash your hands and faces, and Laurie, would you please set the table for four?"

"What's left for you to do?" Laurie pouted.

"I'm heating the sauce right now," he said, setting a pan on the stove. "It can simmer while we go and get Molly!"

"Do you like Molly?" Kim asked her uncle.

Mitch smiled down at her. "I sure do, Kim."

Eyes bright, Kim asked, "Do you like her better than you liked Joy?"

Mitch was silent. He had hoped the girls had forgotten about Joy. The ending of their affair had been abrupt. Until he had met Molly, he hadn't been sure he was completely over Joy. Now he was sure.

Admiring men call women like Joy a trophy. Beautiful, talented, career oriented and young, she had not taken kindly to Mitch's new role as caretaker of his two nieces. That almost made her a mother, for goodness sake! She was much too young for that role. So Joy gave him the old 'It's not about you, it's about me' speech and walked out of his life.

"Girls," he finally said, "you'll find as you get older that you are capable of liking lots of people."

"But I really liked Joy," wailed Kim. "She watched cartoons with me all the time. Will Molly watch cartoons with me?"

Mitch ruffled Kim's hair. "I'll just bet she might. Why don't you ask her tonight? It's time to go get Molly. Everyone into the car and buckle up. Laurie, will you help Kim?"

At exactly five o'clock, Mitch pulled into Molly's driveway. The girls giggled their way from the car to the porch. They had been excited all day, snickering and whispering to each other about Uncle Mitch's new girlfriend. They had plans for tonight. Both of them had picked their favorite toy to share with Molly when they showed her their bedrooms.

He rang the doorbell. "Did either of you hear the bell? I didn't."

"Ring it again, Uncle Mitch!" urged Kim.

"I don't think the doorbell's working," offered Laurie.

"Guess she didn't get it fixed," Mitch looked annoyed. "I'll have to knock then."

So knock Mitch did. In fact, he pounded. Laurie cupped her hands around her eyes and peered into the living room. "I think I see her. She's sitting in a big chair, but she's not coming to the door!"

"I see her! I see her!" shouted Kim. "She moved!"

Mitch, frowning in frustration, asked, "Is she coming to the door?"

"I don't think so. She just moved her head."

Mitch was stunned. What was going on? "Is she looking at us?"

Kim cried, "I don't think she wants to see us! Why is she doing this, Uncle Mitch?"

"Didn't she know we were coming?" Laurie asked, near tears. "Didn't you tell her the time?"

Mitch felt a pang in his heart, "Yes, I did," He cupped his hands around his eyes and peered through the window in time to see Molly turn her head away from the door.

"Molly! Molly!" shouted the girls.

He pounded on the door one last time, and then they turned and walked back to the car.

Mitch didn't know what to think. Maybe Molly was having second thoughts. Maybe Molly had thought it over and, like Joy, decided that she wanted nothing to do with a man saddled with two little girls. Maybe he had Molly figured out all wrong. Maybe she didn't want a relationship after all...at least not with him.

The ride home was a quiet one. All day long, he had pictured in his mind what the evening would be like. In his imagination, they were all around the table, laughing and eating spaghetti. He had smiled at the thought that Laurie would mess up her shirt with spaghetti sauce, and Molly would probably do the same. At least, he had thought, she won't have on one of my ties to mess up.

Driving home alone with the sobbing girls in the back seat was not what he had pictured.

Chapter 24

MITCH AND THE GIRLS looked at the spaghetti sauce still simmering on the stove. It was hard to believe that in such a short time everything had changed.

Kim wrinkled her nose. "Uncle Mitch, could I please have macaroni and cheese instead of spaghetti? I don't think my tummy wants spaghetti right now."

"I think we all feel the same way, Kim. I'll start the water boiling for the noodles, and then I have to make two phone calls."

His first call was to May's parents. Joseph and Kiersten were at first hesitant about getting the girls a week early. After briefly considering it, they quickly embraced the idea and told Mitch they would see him and the girls later that evening.

His second call was to Captain Hilburn.

"Detective Hatch, here, sir."

"What can I do for you, Detective?" asked the Captain.

"Earlier today I told you that I wanted to go next week for my training, but something has come up. I would like to go this week instead. Would that be a problem?"

"No problem," the captain assured him. "But could you be ready to go tomorrow morning?"

"What are the arrangements?" Mitch asked.

"Be at the station by six-thirty with your bags packed," said the captain. "A bus will take all the new personnel to our training center."

"Where would that be?" Mitch was wondering why he even asked the question. It didn't matter to him where the bus was going to take him. He just wanted to get far away from here; maybe the bus would take him to a place where his heart didn't hurt.

"A bit north of the bridge in the Upper Peninsula" was the reply.

"Any special thing I should pack?" Mitch asked.

"Bring mostly casual and outdoor clothes. Some of the training sessions are done in the Marquette National Forest. And, Detective Hatch, where you're going has no cell tower nearby, so you'll be out of communication with the world for a week. Will that be a problem?"

It surprised him how much it hurt to think that Molly wouldn't know or even care that he would be gone for a week. "I'll be at the station tomorrow morning."

Over macaroni and cheese, he told the still subdued girls they were going to Grandpa and Grandma Westin's house a week early and they would be going right after they finished eating.

"Why tonight, Uncle Mitch?" Kim pleaded, "Why can't we go tomorrow morning?"

"Because early tomorrow morning I have to go away for a week's training. Remember the hard test I took to become a detective? Well now I have to go away and learn how to be a good detective."

"But you're already a good detective!" cried Laurie. "I heard you talking to Grandpa Hatch. You told him that you helped catch some real bad people!"

"That's true, but I still have to go for more training."

"A whole week?" squealed Laurie. "What if we don't like it at their house? We've never stayed there before. Why can't we go to Grandpa Hatch's house?"

"Because your mother's parents want to spend time with you, too." He gave them both a loving pat on the back. "Now, no more talk. Go upstairs and start packing. Put in enough clothes for six days. Don't forget your favorite books and toys. I'll be in to check on you as soon as I finish packing my own bag. I want to leave here in thirty minutes."

Reshaping next week's activities had helped keep the pain of Molly's rejection in the back of his mind. Now that he had ironed out all the details for a fast get away, the pain returned. It was his own fault, he thought. He had wanted something good to come out of this relationship, but obviously, Molly hadn't felt the same way. And springing his two charges on her with no warning had been a big mistake.

What was done, was done. He picked up his cell phone and, by habit, started to put it into his pocket. Since Captain Hilburn had said there were no towers where they were going, there was no reason to take the phone. He turned off the phone and laid it on the bathroom counter.

Kim, thinking she might need something to comfort her in the coming week, was stuffing her blanket into her backpack when she spied Uncle Mitch's phone. She dropped it into the pack and smiled in anticipation of the surprised look on his face when she handed it to him.

"All packed, girls? I'll bet you both forgot your toothbrushes."

Both girls chimed, "No, we didn't,"

"Good girls!" Mitch hugged his two nieces. "I'm proud of you. I'll bring the suitcases and you both go get into the car. Laurie, help Kim buckle up in the car seat. Grandma and Grandpa Westin, ready or not, here we come!"

Chapter 25

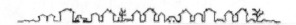

MOLLY SLEPT SOUNDLY in Dave's favorite chair. Fleeting images surfaced in her dream state, only to be replaced by snatches of others. She smiled at a very pleasant dream of helping her father build a doghouse for the puppy she had received at her sixth birthday party. In her dream, she heard her father pounding in the nails that fastened the nameplate "Roscoe" to the finished house.

Finally, she awoke and sat up in the chair. The luminous dial of a digital clock on top of the television set showed 5:00.

That was the best nap ever! She felt as if she'd had a whole night's sleep, but it had just been fifteen minutes. However, she was puzzled to notice it was dark outside. Dark at five o'clock? In summer, Northern Michigan enjoys long hours of daylight. Was someone playing a joke on her?

She jumped out of the chair and ran through the house, looking for an explanation for her confusion.

Reality finally hit her like a sledgehammer. She hadn't slept just fifteen minutes. In her exhausted state, she had slept twelve hours and fifteen minutes.

Her hand flew to her mouth in horror. What had she done? Had Mitch and the girls tried to wake her? How was she ever going to explain this?

She picked up the phone, and then put it back down; it was much too early. Later she would call him and arrange to meet him…maybe for lunch. Something this awful had to be discussed face to face. Would he even agree to meet her?

How could she have done this? Wave after wave of regret washed over her. It startled her to realize how much she had been looking forward to being with Mitch. She cried when she thought of the spaghetti dinner that never happened.

Even in her frustrated state, she marveled at the fact that she had slept through the entire night. When was the last time she had done that? Why, oh why, did she have to do it last night?

By seven o'clock, she was ready for the day. She was standing by the door, keys in her hand, when she realized she had no place to go. Clara wouldn't be at work for two more hours. That empty office would be worse than being here at home. Strange. She had never before felt lonely in her own house. Mitch and the girls had filled her home with something that she hadn't even known was missing...until it was gone. Now, because of her damn legs, it might never be there again.

Wandering around from room to room, she tried in vain to find an activity to occupy her mind until Clara opened the office. Failing to find any, she kicked off her shoes and stretched out on her bed.

CLARA'S CALL FROM the office woke her at nine-thirty.

"Molly," Clara scolded, "what are you doing home at this hour? Sounds like I woke you, too."

"Yes, you did. I can't believe I fell asleep!" Molly sobbed. "Clara, the most awful thing happened last night!"

Clara paused for a bit, debating if she really wanted to hear the awful thing that happened last night. Curiosity won. "Was Mitch's spaghetti that bad?"

"I never had the chance to find out!" Molly wailed.

"Well, then, what? Did he stand you up? Want me to put out a contract on him? I have names."

"No, nothing like that," Molly said with a sigh. "I was ready fifteen minutes early, so I sat down in Dave's big easy chair and fell asleep."

Clara nodded, remembering. She had fallen asleep in that chair, too. "So, why didn't they wake you up?"

"For one thing, the doorbell never has worked. I meant to get it fixed, but I didn't," she lamented. "I pulled the chair over by the window so that I could see them on the porch."

Clara thought for a bit and then said quietly, "That means they could see you, too."

"That's what I'm afraid of. If they saw me there in the chair and not getting up to answer the door...I can't imagine what they thought."

"Molly, you best get on that phone and call Mitch. If you ever had to make 'nice, nice' it's now!"

"I'm going to call his office right now. I guess I should thank you for waking me." Changing the subject, she asked, "Anything happening at the office?"

"Mrs. Ruby Blair, the seller on Elizabeth Street, wants you to call her," answered Clara. "Do you have her number?"

"I have the file here at home. That's the house that had the gas leak. She probably wants to thank me for taking care of the problem while the family was out of town."

"I hate to tell you this, but she didn't sound like she was calling to thank you for anything."

"Wonder what she has to be unhappy about. Oh, well, I'll get to her after I call Mitch. Bye."

She got a recorded message when she called him at the station. A puzzled Molly heard Mitch say that he would be out of the office until next Monday.

A call to his cell phone got a recording telling her to leave a message. She didn't leave one.

Frustration was making Molly frantic. How could she apologize to Mitch and straighten out this whole mess if she couldn't talk to him?

There has to be a good reason Mitch was out of touch. Maybe it was a family problem. Remembering his dad's biking accident, she spent some time convincing herself that the problem had to do with his dad. She knew better; she was the cause. How rejected all of them must feel! To see her sitting there, apparently watching them, but not answering the door. How much worse could it be? Bitter tears of regret coursed down her cheeks.

She blew her nose, wiped her eyes, and called the owner of her Elizabeth Street listing just to get her mind off Mitch.

"Mrs. Blair? Molly Allen here. My secretary said you wanted me to call."

"Well," Mrs. Blair answered without pleasantries, "it took you long enough!"

"I'm sorry, Mrs. Blair. Is something wrong?"

"Something wrong?" Mrs. Blair snorted. "I should say so!"

Molly steeled herself before she replied. "How can I help?"

"I want to know just how many men tramped through my house while I was gone!"

Clara was right. It didn't sound like Mrs. Blair was calling to thank her for the entire afternoon she had spent taking care of a gas leak. "Are you talking about the men from the gas company?"

"I would hope so!" Mrs. Blair paused, and then asked suspiciously, "Were there other men who went through my house that I should know about?"

"What's the problem, Mrs. Blair?"

"What's the problem, you ask?" her voice was unsteady. "I'll tell you what the problem is! They wrecked my new carpet, that's what!"

"Oh my! What did they do to your carpet?"

"Grease!" shouted Mrs. Blair. "Grease! One of them had grease on his shoes, and I can trace everywhere he traipsed through my house!"

"I guess we should be calling the gas company to see if they have insurance coverage for their workers. Would you like me to call them?"

"No, I don't want you to do anything. In fact, I don't want you listing my house anymore!"

Molly couldn't believe what she was hearing. "But this is not my fault. Your house had a gas leak and I sat outside for several hours until the problem was fixed."

"You sat outside?" There was a sharp intake of breath, a pause, and then in a steely voice Mrs. Blair asked. "Are you telling me you left those men alone in my house?"

"Mrs. Blair," pleaded Molly, "please understand that they wouldn't allow me to go into a dangerous situation. So no, I was not in the house with them."

"That does it! You allowed unsupervised strangers in my house! I want my listing back!"

"But the contract you signed is for two more months. I've worked hard to sell your house. Not only have I paid for ads, I've held your house open several Sundays."

"I don't want you listing my house!" Then her voice softened. "Anyway, my niece just got her real estate license and I think she will do a better job because she's family."

"All right." Molly gave up. "Come to my office tomorrow, and I'll have the papers prepared to terminate the contract. Good day, Mrs. Blair."

Molly felt sick to her stomach. What else could happen today?

The phone rang.

Molly, still shaken from the last call, answered with a tenuous voice. "Hello?"

"Miss Allen?"

"Yes."

"This is Norma Lacy, the owner of the condo in Slagle's Corner."

Molly smiled with relief. She and Norma had enjoyed a cup of coffee together after one Sunday open house; this was going to be a good call. "Good morning, Mrs. Lacy!"

"That's easy for you to say!"

"Easy for me to say good morning?" Molly, puzzled, asked slowly. "Why would you say that?"

"Because a cat hasn't peed on your bed!"

Molly's forehead puckered. "Pardon me?"

Mrs. Lacy raised her voice. "I said, because a cat hasn't peed on your bed!"

"That's right, because I don't have a cat."

"It's all your fault!" Norma Lacy's voice was getting higher. "You gave someone permission to go through my condo while I was away."

"But wasn't that the arrangement we made?" Molly was speaking softly in an attempt to calm Mrs. Lacy. "You want buyers to see your condo, don't you? How do you expect to sell it if no one looks at it?"

"Well, I guess so. But the last agent who showed it shut the door to the basement. When Cuddles couldn't get downstairs to go in his litter box, he used my bed the whole week end!"

"How awful! But what happened to the sign?"

"What sign?"

"Come on, Mrs. Lacy, don't tell me you didn't do it."

Mrs. Lacy didn't reply.

Molly prodded. "I distinctly remember telling you, and I have it in my notes, to put a sign on the basement door. Without that sign, how is anyone supposed to know that the door should remain open for Cuddles to get down to his litter box? Your cat hides every time someone comes to the door so no one even knows that a cat lives in the condo."

"Miss Allen, I don't care what you say. I demand that you make this right!"

"Please be reasonable, Mrs. Lacy," implored Molly. "How can I make something right that I didn't cause?"

"I am calling my lawyer. I want a new mattress, a new bedspread, and new pillows!"

"And I am calling the Humane Society!"

"The Humane Society?" Mrs. Lacy's voice shook with rage. "How the hell did they get into this conversation?"

Molly took a deep breath and yelled, "Because you were cruel to your cat, that's why!"

Mrs. Lacy shouted back, "How dare you! I love Cuddles!"

"But not enough to put that sign on the door," Molly persisted. "He was in misery all weekend because he couldn't get to his box."

"That does it!" screeched Mrs. Lacy. "On top of the new bedding, I want my listing back! I don't want you to have anything more to do with my condo!"

"Mrs. Lacy!" Molly said in a more controlled voice. "Let's talk this over!"

"I'll be in tomorrow to sign off the listing contract! Good bye! And I don't care if you have a good day or not!" Molly cringed at the noise of a slammed receiver.

Molly slid off her chair and sat on the floor. Maybe she should just get into the car and drive away before the phone had a chance to ring again.

The phone rang. What else could happen?

She answered cautiously. "Hello?"

"Hey Molly, this is Mr. Wise! I called the office and your secretary said to try you at home."

"Oh, hello, Mr. Wise!" she smiled with relief. "You don't know how nice it is to hear a friendly voice!"

"Why? Have you been hearing unfriendly voices this early in the morning?"

"Unfortunately, yes. But, if you're calling to see if there are any new apartments on the market today, I guess I don't have to tell you that I haven't as yet gone to the office. Am I hearing a happy note in your voice?"

He laughed. "You can tell from my voice? How about that? Yes, I am happy! I found an apartment."

"You found it on your own?" she asked. "Do you want me to make an appointment and take you through it?"

"No, you don't understand!" His voice resounded with happiness. "You don't have to take me through it because I've already signed the papers. I move in tomorrow!"

"I still don't understand," Molly replied.

"The man I'm replacing was trying to sublet his apartment. The apartment is furnished and I snatched it up. He hadn't mentioned it to me because he knew I was bringing my family from Grand Rapids, but you and I know how that went." He paused, sighed, and went on. "I don't even have to buy kitchen utensils or bedding for that matter. I can't believe my luck!"

"How very fortunate for you, Mr. Wise," she replied sweetly, hoping he didn't hear the sarcasm in her voice. Yeah, she thought, fortunate for you; I don't get a commission for all my work. Sometimes this job is just a stinking pile of...

Mr. Wise interrupted her thoughts. "I just called to tell you I don't need your services any more. But, I also wanted to tell you that I enjoyed the time we spent together. Even though you didn't find me this apartment, I appreciate how hard you worked for me."

Molly bit her tongue. "I appreciate your saying that."

After a pause, Mr. Wise asked, "Now that I'm no longer one of your customers, would you feel differently about my dinner and movie invitation?"

Molly sputtered. "Mr. Wise," she managed to say in a pleasant voice, "you may not be my customer any more, but you're still a married man. So, no, there will be no dinner and movie. Bye!"

With that, she grabbed her keys and ran out the door.

Chapter 26

CLARA, TODAY RESPLENDENT in a sapphire caftan, was filing her shiny pink nails when Molly made a dramatic entrance into the office. In her haste, she caught the belt of her coat on the doorknob and spun around, trying to free it.

"Wow! That was quite an entrance! Too bad there's no one here to appreciate the artistry of that triple spin. I'd give it an '8' myself."

"Clara, be serious!" moaned Molly as she freed herself. "I'm in deep trouble."

Clara's pencil-thin plucked eyebrows shot up. "Who with?"

"Just about everybody, give or take a few."

Clara dropped the nail file. "Come on, girl! It can't be that bad!"

Molly's coat sailed through the air and puddled at the bottom of the coat rack. "Wanna bet?"

"Let's start with the worst one," Clara said, getting into the mood of the game. "What trouble would that be?"

"The worst one?" Molly sighed deeply, "The Mitch trouble hurts the most. Let's start with that one."

"You said you never made it to the spaghetti dinner because you slept and they couldn't wake you from your nap. You sound like Sleeping Beauty! Maybe Prince Charming will kiss you and make it all nice again?"

"This is no fairy tale, Clara," she said as she brushed away a tear that was making its way down her cheek. "This is for real, and it really hurts!"

"You never told me what happened when you called him to make 'nice, nice'"

Molly choked back a sob. "It never happened."

Surprised, Clara asked, "Wouldn't he talk to you? Is he that angry?"

"I don't know what he's feeling because he's out of contact."

"Out of contact since last night? How can that be?" Clara shook her head firmly. "He has baggage! He can't go anywhere without those little girls, and going out of contact that quickly takes some planning; he didn't have time for planning."

"Well, his machine at work says he will be gone for a week, and his cell phone is in the old 'leave a message' mode."

Clara was quiet for a bit, trying, but failing to come up with a solution. "Now that's a hard one to figure. Let's look at another one of your troubles that might be easier to solve."

"You have a choice. Wanna hear what the greasy feet of one of the gas workers did to Ruby Blair's new carpet? Or, would you rather hear about the cat that used Norma Lacy's bed for a litter box all weekend? Or, how about good old friendly Mr. Wise who, after dropping me as his agent, asked me out for dinner and a movie? Now that's a good one."

Clara listened in disbelief as Molly related the stories. "What a morning you're having, and it's only ten o'clock! Let's see. What's left is good old friendly Mr. Wise. Do I hear a sarcastic note in your voice?"

"Good old friendly Mr. Wise called to thank me for all my help, but said he didn't need my services anymore because he'd found a furnished apartment on his own. The deal is all signed, sealed, and he moves in tomorrow." Molly sighed. "Sometimes, working solely on commission sucks. People view us as missionaries sent to help them, and it really doesn't matter if we don't get paid for our services."

"And he wanted to date you?" Clara's eyes were wide in disbelief. "I'd been thinking about getting my license, but I doubt that I would survive very long."

"If it weren't for buyers like my two lake houses, I wouldn't survive, either," Molly said quietly.

"Speaking of surviving," Clara teased, "have you forgotten your three o'clock appointment with Jack the Ripper?"

Molly stopped in the rush to her office. She had to call Mitch again and this time she'd leave a message. Showing the farmhouse on Miller Road was the last thing she wanted to do. "Clara, find the listing agent of that property, and tell whoever it is that I need to pick their brain! Have that person call me."

Shutting the door to her office, she sat at her desk and composed, in her head, an explanation to Mitch. How much detail could she squeeze into a message? In the end, she simply said, "Mitch, this is Molly. Please call me so I can explain about last night. I feel awful."

Across town, the cell phone on the bottom of a little girl's backpack was quiet.

Life was certainly going off in strange directions. Trying to get her mind off her problems, she was considering putting her head down on her desk for a nap, when the lister of the farmhouse called.

"Molly, this is Judy Howard of White Realty. I hear you're going to show the farm house!"

"Thanks for calling me back, Judy. A developer from downstate wants to see it today at three o'clock. All I know about that property is what's on the listing ticket. I need to know details."

"I'll share everything I have with you," Judy said. "That property has been on the market for years! I don't know how many other offices in town have had the listing, but no one has managed to sell it. You go, girl! Hey, how did you handle the gas leak in the Blair residence? I couldn't smell gas, but my buyer could."

"That's a story I might tell you over a cup of coffee some day," Molly replied.

"Is it a funny story? Will it make me laugh?"

"Well, I guess it depends on whether you're the listener or the teller. Notice the new listings today? Someone else has the Blair house now. Mrs. Blair took the listing away from me."

"Oh, oh," Judy's voice was full of sympathy. "One of those stories."

"It's a good one, and I think I'll let you buy the coffee while I tell it to you. But, back to the farmhouse. Can you make a packet for me? I'll stop and get it on my way to Miller Road. If I get to the farmhouse early, I'll have time to go over the information and be ready for the buyer. Is there a lockbox?"

"Yes. I'll give you the combination when I see you. Just the thought of maybe getting that old house sold is making me happy!"

Chapter 27

MOLLY SAT QUIETLY at her desk, wondering how she was going to fill the day until her three o'clock appointment; then she had a thought. When a girl's in trouble, who does she need to talk to?

Peggy Allen answered the phone on the first ring.

"Well, Mom," teased Molly, "were you sitting on the phone?"

"Good morning, Molly. No, I wasn't sitting on the phone," Peggy said, amused by the accusation, "but would you believe I was just picking up the phone to call you?"

Concerned, Molly asked, "Is there anything wrong? You have something to tell me?"

"Not really, honey, but you have something to tell me."

"How do you know that?"

Peggy said smugly, "It's just a feeling I've had all morning."

Her mom did things like this so often it made Molly want to hum the Twilight Zone theme song. "Did the feeling include lunch?"

Peggy laughed. "You know it does. And your brother Tom dropped in, so you two can visit while I cook."

Molly snorted. "Yeah, cook! Since when do you have to cook peanut butter and jelly sandwiches? That's lunch, isn't it?"

"You got me there!" Peggy had the grace to admit it. "Be here at noon?"

"Yes. See you!"

THERE WAS ANOTHER CAR parked in the driveway when Molly arrived. Her mother's front door was always unlocked so Molly just walked in.

Tom, his arms waving wildly, was intently talking to her mother. The conversation stopped abruptly. He was obviously telling his mom something that was upsetting. When, some months ago, he told Molly he was training for a new job, his eyebrows had danced up and down like red caterpillars, but he wouldn't tell her what it was. He said he didn't want to jinx it. Molly wondered if this heated conversation with their mom had anything to do with that.

"Oh, hello, Mol," Tom cried as he rushed across the room and hugged her. "It's been a long time!"

"Hi, Little Bro!" Molly hugged him back "And whose fault is it that we don't see much of each other?"

"Probably both of ours," he admitted. "You sure keep busy with that office of yours. Do you make any money?"

"I make enough money to keep the door open and pay Clara. But sometimes this career is very...," she sighed. "I don't know really how to describe the ups and downs in the life of a real estate agent."

"As long as there are more ups than there are downs, you've got it made," Tom reasoned. "I see your signs all over town now."

"You'll be seeing two fewer pretty soon." There was a catch in Molly's voice. "This morning, in the space of twenty minutes, I lost two listings and a lease."

Peggy looked closely at her daughter. "Molly, 'fess up now. Losing business is not what's making you look the way you did when your dog Roscoe died. You've survived periods of bad luck like this before. There's something else going on now, isn't there?"

Tom cupped his ear. "Do I hear strains of Twilight Zone?"

Molly looked surprised. "You've picked up on our mother's psychic abilities?"

"You kidding? When I lived at home, she figured out what was going on in my social life before I did. And, she'd tell me! I had to move out so that I could be surprised by things actually happening without her saying, 'I told you so'!"

"Tom!" Peggy frowned. "That's no way to talk about your mother!"

They were eating lunch when Peggy turned to Molly. "Ready to get what's bothering you off your chest?"

Molly put down her sandwich, cleared her throat, and announced, "Well, I met a guy I think I could really like." She cocked her head and grinned before she imparted the next bit of information. "He's a detective."

Detective? Tom's head jerked.

"Hallelujah!" Peggy shouted. "How did you meet him?"

Molly shook her head. "I'd rather not get into that right now, if you don't mind."

"But I do mind!" Peggy was so excited she clapped her hands. "I want details! How in the world did you meet a detective?"

"Later, Mom! Right now I want to tell you the problem." Molly took a sip of coffee before starting the story. "His name is Mitch. Our first date was going to be special so he picked out a restaurant that had a dress code. I knew I had to wear something dressy."

"What was the name of the restaurant?" asked Peggy.

Molly hung her head. "I never found out."

"And the plot thickens," mused Tom.

"Remember that emerald green dress that I wore that awful night at the dress rehearsal?"

"A beautiful dress!" Peggy's eyes were misty.

Molly agreed. "It is a beautiful dress. Well, it's been in the back of my closet in a dust jacket. I always imagined that the dress had a curse on it, so I never wore it again."

"Now who's weird?" Tom whispered to his mother.

Molly gave them both a dirty look. "Anyhow, I got all dolled up, hair curled and make-up on. I was really looking forward to my first date in three years."

"Three years? My poor baby!" Peggy cried as she grabbed Molly in a bear hug. "I hadn't realized it's been that long."

Extracting herself from Peggy's arms, Molly continued the story. When she got to the part about Mitch arriving with two children in tow, Peggy looked puzzled. "He showed up for your first date with two children? What did you do?"

"I freaked out."

"Without finding out why he had the children with him?" Peggy peered closely at her daughter. "Why would you do that?"

"Why?" Molly's voice quivered. "Why? How can you ask that after what Dave did to me? All that deception? Well, here was another deceiver. Mitch obviously had a wife somewhere and these were his two kids."

"Calm down, Molly, but I admit that would be the first conclusion you would come to. What did you do then?"

"I slammed the door and yelled at him to go back home to his wife!"

"Molly, Molly," Peggy chided her daughter. "There must have been a better way to handle the situation."

"Yes, Mother, there was," Molly said sadly and went on with the story. She finished with, "His sitter for the evening canceled and he had no choice but to bring them along."

"Ah," said Tom, "so that's why you never found out what restaurant he had picked."

"Right. And we did have a real nice evening after everything settled down."

"Nothing is sounding like a problem so far," Peggy said. "I guess there must be more to the story. Anything else happen that night?"

Molly froze. Events of that night slammed into her memory and stunned her. Mom didn't know about the drug runner in her attic.

"Molly, are you all right?" Peggy peered at her daughter. "Whatever happened, it can't be that bad, can it?"

Molly regained her composure; if she had her way, her mother would never learn about the incident. She took a deep breath and returned to the present.

Her eyes filled with tears, "I screwed up big time."

Peggy handed her a paper napkin. Molly blew her nose and continued with the story about the spaghetti dinner that never happened. She told them about falling asleep in Dave's chair and dreaming about the time she and her dad built Roscoe a new doghouse. She got to the part where her dad was pounding Roscoe's name on it when Tom interrupted. "That was Mitch pounding on the door, I'll bet! Could they see you in the chair?"

"Definitely. They saw me sitting there, watching them, and not answering the door. I can't begin to think what must have been going through their minds." Tears ran down her cheeks.

There was a pained look on Peggy's face. "But couldn't you explain what happened?"

"I could if I could reach Mitch," Molly said, rubbing her eyes. "The message on his work phone says that he will be out of the office until next week, and he doesn't answer the messages I leave on his cell phone. I've been frantic."

Tom was closely watching Molly. Could she be the nightwalker that Sammy the Grunt had been looking for? The name of the detective he was working with was Hatch. He was new, and Tom didn't know his first name. But if he was one of the new personnel, right now he probably was in the Upper Peninsula for the week. Tom had chosen to go next week. "Mol, that house that you sold to yourself? Where is it?"

"What does my house have to do with my Mitch problem?" Agitated that he had interrupted her story, she stomped her foot. "You're changing the subject!"

"Sorry. Just wondering. Go on."

"Well," Molly sputtered and then admitted, "I guess I did finish the story. There's no more to tell."

Peggy hugged her. "He has to come back sometime from wherever he went. You're going to have to make him understand that your sleeping was just an unfortunate thing that happened. If he is anything like the man you told me about, he'll forgive you."

"You always make me feel better, Mom!"

"Mol," Tom asked. "Is there a junky alley in your neighborhood?"

"Yes, there is. And there was a double homicide there a few days ago," she answered. "But what made you ask that question?"

"I read about the murders in the paper," Tom hedged, "and it made me wonder if your house might be in that part of town."

Molly felt guilty. She had lived in that house for some time now but she claimed she was always too busy to invite them to visit. So now, smiling, she asked, "How would the two of you like to come for a cookout and see my house for yourselves?"

"We thought you'd never ask!" was the unanimous reply.

Chapter 28

CLARENCE, FACE DOWN on his wet pillow, cringed at the sound of cell doors closing and locks clanking shut. Pretending to be asleep, he tried to ignore Albert, his cellmate.

"Clarence," Albert whispered, "I know you're not asleep."

"Well," came the muffled reply, "I might be if you'd quit botherin' me!"

Albert sighed. "If I had been with you, this wouldn't have happened."

Clarence winced in pain as he tried to turn his head to look at Albert. "Ouch!" he muttered as he put his face back on the pillow.

"Someone stopped the guys that were beating you in the shower. Do you know who it was?" asked Albert. He was curious. Clarence had been the play-object of several bullies ever since the two of them had arrived on the block. For some reason, when Albert was with Clarence the inmates left him alone. But he wasn't with Clarence today when the incident happened. Clarence should be in the infirmary.

"I couldn't see the guy because I was gettin' the crap kicked out of me," Clarence said through clenched teeth.

"Did you hear the guy's voice? I wish you could remember," Albert said quietly. "Someone came to your rescue, and that doesn't make sense. Not in this place."

Clarence painfully turned his head and looked up at Albert. "I think it was Jesus," he whispered.

Albert smothered a snort. "You think Jesus stopped them from beating you?"

"I was praying to Him for help when I heard Him speak!"

"You heard Jesus speak?" Albert's raised eyebrows almost met his black widow's peak.

"Yes, I did," Clarence's battered face brightened. "Jesus said, 'I told you not to do that!' and they stopped kickin' me."

Albert gently patted Clarence's head. Jail was no place for someone as simple as Clarence whose only crime had been hanging with the wrong crowd. "That sure sounds like somethin' Jesus would say," he agreed. "Think you're gonna be able to sleep?"

"If I don't move, I don't hurt," came the muffled reply.

"If you can't move in the morning, you're gonna have to have someone look at your injuries," Albert said.

"Not the infirmary, Albert! Please! The last time I was there it was really bad!" Clarence whimpered.

"I know it was," Albert agreed. "I heard through the grapevine that they fired that guard."

"How do we know that someone just as bad didn't get his job?" Clarence looked at Albert through the slit of one swollen eye.

"We don't," Albert had to agree. A half smile crossed his face as he looked at his bloodied cellmate. "Maybe Jesus will talk to the guard at the infirmary."

Albert tucked the covers around Clarence, surprised by the depth of his protective feelings toward this innocent, child-like man. He retreated to his own bunk. Sobs that turned to deep sighs and then to regular breathing told him Clarence was asleep. The quiet cell gave Albert time to reflect on the events of the past week. Clarence's life had been hell from day one. Bullies had spotted an easy target the moment they laid eyes on him, but someone with authority had stopped them today.

Mulling over all the possibilities, Albert soon fell asleep and was dreaming. His dream of a warm sun and freedom were just that, a dream. Because of the sentence's length for the McGuire Alley murders, a warm sun and freedom were years away.

Chapter 29

LUNCH WITH TOM AND MOM had been just a diversion; the knot in her stomach had not diminished in size. Sighing, she dialed the office.

"Allen Real Estate, may I help you?" asked Clara.

"Hey, Clara, it's me. I'm on my way to pick up the information on the farm house and then on to the three o'clock appointment."

"Say hello to Jack the Ripper for me," snickered Clara.

"I know you checked up on this guy, but just in case, I think we need to do our famous code game."

"Gotcha. You call me when you get there, and then every fifteen minutes after that I call you. If everything's fine, you can just say everything's fine. Now what are you going to say if it's not fine?"

"You mean besides 'help'?" Molly laughed. "How about 'everything is excellent'. The word 'excellent' will mean the guy is really Jack the Ripper and I need help. Clara, you and your names! I'm still having trouble looking at Mitch and not thinking Mr. Eye Candy." Molly's voice trailed off. Just mentioning Mitch's name tightened the knot. "Clara, I'm at Judy Howard's office. She's the one who has the listing on the farmhouse. I'm getting a free cup of coffee when I tell her what happened to my Blair listing; you know, the one where Judy's buyer smelled gas."

"That story's worth more than a cup of coffee. I'd go for at least a donut or two if I were you!" chuckled Clara. "Good luck, and don't forget to call me when you get to the farmhouse," she said, ending the call.

MOLLY PULLED OFF the highway and followed the overgrown, rutted road that ran through neglected acres of decaying and unharvested crops. Almost hidden by tall weeds, rusted farm equipment dotted the fields, doomed to sit forever on the spot where someone had abandoned them. The farmhouse, when it finally appeared, seemed to be leaning toward the sagging barn as if it were trying to find comfort in this isolated setting.

Part of the porch had fallen away and what was left was rotted. The railing, when she touched it, came off in her hand. If the rest of the house was as bad as the porch, she could only imagine what she would find inside. Why was Henry Baker interested in seeing the inside of a house that would be torn down if he developed the property?

Coaxing the key to turn in the rusty lock took time and determination. With a protesting groan, the door opened and Molly found herself standing in a musty museum. Roof leaks had dissolved plastered walls. Wallpaper, faded and torn, hung in shreds. Drapes at the windows were limp and chewed, probably by the vermin she could hear scurrying around.

With a growing sense of dread, Molly called the office. Before Clara could get out her greeting, Molly cut her off. "It's me, Clara."

"Is Henry Baker with you?" Clara asked.

"No, and I'm getting a bad feeling about this. I'm inside the house and I really wish I didn't have to be here. The house is fully furnished. It looks like it's just waiting for the owners to return.

There's someone's reading glasses on a side table, and an apron is thrown over a kitchen chair. UCK!"

"What happened?"

"Uh, it was only a mouse, a little one at that, but it scared me," Molly shuddered. "Hey, wait a minute! There are dishes in the sink!"

"So the lady of the house didn't wash the dishes before she walked out. Big deal!"

"Nice try, Clara, but the food on these dishes is fresh. I'm getting a bad feeling about this house. Do you know the creepy feeling you get when someone is watching you?"

"Come on, Molly, you're scaring me now!"

"You're not the only one. Something bad happened in this house; I can feel it! Call Judy Howard. The sellers have to disclose anything that happened if it might be unacceptable to a buyer."

"I'm looking at the listing ticket, Molly. The bank owns that property."

"Then see if you can find anyone who knows what happened here. I'm going outside to wait for Henry. Call me in fifteen." Molly ended the call and slipped her cell phone into a jacket pocket.

She stood for a moment at the sink looking out the window at the fields. In her imagination, she could envision the woman of the house doing this several times a day. Molly closed her eyes and tried to put herself in the woman's shoes. *What would my days be like isolated out here away from everything? Do I love my husband? Am I happy? Do I have friends?* Suddenly, Molly's eyes flew open. The woman she was pretending to be was frightened! The shared feeling of impending death was so strong that Molly grabbed the edge of the sink for support. Something terrible had happened to this woman!

EVELYN ALLEN HARPER

Molly was so intent with her thoughts that her reaction to seeing the window reflect movement behind her was too slow. She whirled around, but not in time to see who pulled a hood over her head and roughly shoved her into the pantry.

Molly screamed. The pantry door slammed shut before she gathered her wits together, and when she heard the sound of a heavy piece of furniture being wedged against the door, she knew that, for real, she had made an appointment with Jack-the-Ripper. Snatching the hood off her head, she held her breath and listened intently. Her heart was beating so loudly that if anything *was* happening on the other side of the door, she'd have trouble hearing it. The grating sound of the front door as it opened and closed told her she was alone.

It was pitch-black in the pantry. Panic closed down all her thoughts. She stood, frozen in place, the feeling of doom shutting off all her senses. It took a creature running across her shoes to snap her into reality. A few pushes on the door told her whatever was jammed in front of it wasn't going to budge.

With a shaking hand, she pulled her cell phone out of her pocket and, using its light, surveyed her prison. The shelves were lined with jars of home-canned vegetables, and shredded cereal boxes, long emptied by vermin. A glob of solidified slime was all that was left of a basket of potatoes. Molly wrinkled her nose and hit speed-dial

"Hey, the fifteen minutes aren't up!" Clara declared as she answered. "I'm supposed to call you, remember?"

"Help! Oh my God! Oh my God!" Molly sobbed.

"Is this a joke, Boss? What's with this 'Oh my God' bit? You're supposed to say the code word 'excellent'…"

"This is not a joke! I need help fast before he comes back!"

"Who comes back?"

"Probably Jack-the-Ripper! I'm locked in a pantry! Oh my God! Call 911 and get them here fast!"

Clara's bantering ceased. "Molly, I'm on it."

After making the 911 call, the next call Clara made was to Molly's mother. Clara knew she was the one person who could comfort Molly after such an experience.

TIME PASSED VERY slowly in the pitch-dark closet. She shuddered as light from her cell phone glistened off dangling spider webs. Just as the phone went into energy saving mode and the light dimmed, scratches on the wall caught her eye. She closed the phone and opened it again. A stronger light showed the scratches were letters. She recognized 'hep' before the light dimmed. Not wanting to use all the power in her phone, she reached out and traced the deep scratches. Indeed, there was a letter between the 'e' and the 'p'. Was it an 'l'? Turning the phone back on, she was able to see clearly the word 'help' that had been carved into the pantry wall. Help? Had someone else been a prisoner in this pantry?

It seemed like a long time before she heard cars pulling up to the house. The grinding noise of the front door and then the welcome voices of men, probably the police, told her she was safe. The heavy piece of furniture groaned as it was pulled aside and Molly's push on the pantry door opened it.

Try as she might to keep her composure, the sight of her mom and Clara running toward her did her in. Peggy Allen hugged the sobbing daughter who hadn't clung so tightly to her since childhood.

"Oh, Molly" Clara sobbed, "I got you into this! If something had happened to you, I'd never forgive myself!"

The two police officers had stepped back to allow the reunion; now it was their turn. "We have questions about what happened here, but Ma'am," one said, turning to Clara, "what did you mean when you said you got Miss Allen into this?"

"I did investigative work, but I guess I'm not very good at it," Clara sobbed. "The man who wanted to see this property was supposedly a developer from downstate. He said his name was Henry Baker, and he gave me references." She paused, wiped her eyes, and continued. "I called them all, and everyone I talked to had good things to say about the man and his developments."

"Obviously, the man wasn't Henry Baker. Miss Allen, can you give us a description of who did this to you?" The question was asked by the younger of the two police officers. The other one was off searching the house.

"No, I can't," Molly said, still wrapped in her mother's arms, "I just got a brief glimpse of the reflection in the kitchen window. I turned around but whoever it was put a hood over my head before I got a look. I have no idea who it was. You're going to ask me if I have any enemies, if I've sold a house to someone who isn't happy with the transaction, or if I have a disgruntled lover. I can answer no to all of those questions. There is one thing, though. I've been getting a lot of telephone calls with just someone breathing on the other end."

"Now that's something we could work with," the officer said. "How long has this been going on?"

Molly looked at Clara for help. Clara shrugged and said, "Probably just the past few weeks. I get them at the office, too."

"Miss Allen, do you get any of them on your cell phone?" he asked.

"No, come to think of it, the calls are on my home or the office phone. Why, is that important?"

"If it's someone from your past, chances are they wouldn't have your cell phone number. Me, I get a new number every time I switch carriers."

"Based on that, the person would be someone from at least two years ago," Molly figured.

"Miss Allen, work on that line of thinking. In the meantime, we'll pull the phone records for both your home and office and see if that leads us anywhere, but I'm worried about you. What happened here would have sent most women into hysterics. You are almost too calm. Are you sure you're all right?"

Molly gave her mom one last hug and stepped away. "I think so. What I really want to do right now is get away from this house. Something bad happened in here, I don't know what, but I felt it. The hair on my arms actually stood up, and that was before I got locked in the pantry." She shuddered and rubbed her arms.

Returning from his search of the house, the older officer joined the group in time to hear Molly's statement. "She's right," he said. "Something really bad did happen in this house. Of the four people who lived here, the only one who is still alive and out there somewhere, is the son. He murdered his mother, and when his father and younger brother heard the shot, they left their machines in the field and ran to the house. He killed them, too."

The three women had huddled together. "You mean that son was never caught? He's still out there somewhere?"

"Nope, never caught. There was a will that left the farm to him, the oldest son, but since taxes were never paid, the bank owns it."

"How old would this son be now, and what's his name?" Molly shivered as she remembered the sense of death she had felt while pretending to be the woman of the house.

"Let's see." The area between the officer's eyes formed a V as he pondered the question. "If I've figured right, Jerry Miller would be about forty years old right now."

The young officer asked, "Did you find anything when you went through the house?"

"Someone has been spending time here, that's for sure. They've been sleeping in one of the upstairs bedrooms."

"Did you find any evidence of a break-in?"

"None," replied the older one. "No broken windows, no loose boards, and no unlocked doors."

"So," the young one figured, "someone had a key."

"This property has been listed by almost every real estate office in town so I would imagine there are several keys to this place floating around," Molly informed them.

"I suppose that's true, but let's think about someone else who might just have a key," the young officer said.

"It sounds like you have someone in mind," ventured Molly.

His face was aglow with his newfound insight. "How about Jerry Miller, the long lost son coming back to claim his inheritance?"

His announcement was met with silence. "A murderer coming back to claim an inheritance?" the older cop finally asked. "I don't think so."

Molly chimed in. "And how, pray tell, could I have a connection with Jerry Miller? All this happened before my time. I was teaching school when all this went down and my dad was still alive running Allen Real Estate. If this man is Jerry Miller, why would he lure *me* to this house?"

The enthusiasm went out of the young man's voice. "I haven't figured that part out yet."

Molly hesitated before she asked, "Do you think whoever it was planned on coming back...to hurt me?"

"Doesn't look that way to me," the older one said. "There's evidence from dusty footprints that someone was following your progress through the house, watching you the whole time."

"I knew I felt eyes on me!" she cringed, hugging herself. "So if someone was watching me, they saw me talking on my cell phone."

"You and I are thinking the same way, Molly," nodded the older officer. "If whoever it was really wanted to harm you, they'd have taken your cell phone away because they knew you'd call for help."

"So," Molly concluded, "he was just trying to scare me?"

"Looks that way."

Molly grimaced. "Well, he sure did a good job of that!"

AFTER THE POLICE LEFT, the women walked slowly to their cars. The mood was solemn until Clara lightened it when she cackled, "Molly, if Judy Howard is willing to buy you a cup of coffee just to hear your Blair-greasy-shoe story, I think you should hold out for a steak dinner before you tell her what happened today at her farmhouse listing!"

Chapter 30

FOR MOLLY, THE WEEK PASSED very slowly. The phone didn't ring with calls from other agencies to show her listings. No new buyers knocked on her door. Most of the time she huddled in her office behind the closed door, cringing when she was mentally swept back to that dark pantry with the blocked entrance. The police had found nothing in the house or the property that shed any light on the incident, and phone records showed the silent calls had been made from a throwaway cell phone.

Clara, with nothing to do, was taking some time off work. It was spring break and her daughter, Jill, needed someone to be with her two children while she and her husband worked. Jill's two daughters, Emma and Hannah, were delighted that Grandma Clara was going to be with them for the break.

With Clara out of the office, Molly hated to go to work in the morning. Her life had become much too quiet. She had tried to call Mitch several times, but she had even stopped doing that. Ruby Blair and Norma Lacy had both been in the office to sign the listing release. That was the extent of the week's real estate business.

Closing the door to her office early in the afternoon, she walked to the car with her head down, dreading the drive home to a quiet house, a house that had never seemed quiet before. Mitch and the girls had filled her house with warmth. How had she never noticed the crushing silence of her lonely existence?

Thinking about Mitch, even though it hurt, was better than revisiting the locked pantry. But, unbidden, her mind dragged her back to that dark prison. As she started the car to head for home, her heart pounded and her breathing became ragged as she relived the panicky feelings. Who would do such a thing to her? Why? There were so many unanswered questions. Did he plan to come back, or did he intentionally leave her there knowing she had a cell phone to call for help? Deep in thought, the thumping sound of something terribly wrong brought her back to reality. She had a flat tire.

GEORGE TAYLOR, THE OWNER of the town's only garage, was one of Molly's old customers. She had sold George and his wife a little Cape Cod last year. Within minutes of Molly's call for help, George arrived in his tow truck.

"George, am I glad to see you!" she managed a grin. "I have a really flat tire! It's not just out of air, it's flat!"

"Hi, there, Molly! Good to see you again. The wife keeps saying we should have you over for dinner some time so you can see what we've done with the house!" he said as he crouched to look at the tire.

"I'd love that, George."

He straightened up. "Molly," he said in a quiet voice. "This tire is more than flat. It's been slashed."

Molly looked skeptically at him. "Slashed? My tire's slashed? That's crazy!"

"Crazy or not, that's what it is."

"But who would do that to me?" Molly wailed.

"Sell a house to someone who's not happy with his purchase?" he asked. Molly watched George's mouth move, but her brain had shut off all sound.

"You all right?" George asked. "You don't look so good."

Molly gasped, "Oh, George, I just want to go home! The spare tire's in the trunk. Just change the tire and I'll drop by the garage tomorrow and buy a new one."

George shrugged and went to work. "I think you should stop at the police station and tell them about your tire. Maybe it's just kids, but I don't think so. Slashing a tire is pretty malicious."

Molly stopped at the police station and reported the slashed tire. Hoping to find a familiar face, she looked, but didn't see the officers who had responded to the farmhouse fiasco. A disinterested clerk behind the desk took her report. She couldn't help wondering if Mitch, wherever he was, knew what was happening to her. The crushing realization that even if he knew, he wouldn't care, sent her running out of the station holding back tears that were shed unabashedly in her car.

DINNER CAME FROM the freezer, but it really didn't matter; her stomach refused to accept more than a few bites. There was nothing she wanted to see on television, and she had read every book in the stack she had brought home from the library.

As the night dragged on, she sat down at the computer and pulled up her story. No matter how hard she tried, her mind couldn't get into it. Instead, the details of the tragic and unsolved murders of the Miller family filled her head. A local artist had produced an enhanced picture of what, in his opinion, Jerry Miller would look like at age forty. The sight of that picture in the morning paper had given Molly a creepy feeling. The generic picture of Jerry looked like any number of local men.

Pushing all thoughts of Mitch, the pantry, Jerry Miller and the slashed tire out of her head, she tapped her fingers on the computer keys and started typing.

Her new plot was about McGuire's Alley. In her story, terrorists had taken over Old Man McGuire's house, tied him up in one of the bedrooms, and were making a bomb in the garage that was down by the junked car. Christina was the name of the girl in her story.

She typed:

With an earthshaking noise, the alley was lit up with an explosion so violent the air was filled with pieces of McGuire's junk blown higher than the surrounding houses. Heat from the explosion hit her back about the same time a chunk off the old car hit her head.

Molly stopped typing. With a bump on the head like that, Christina was going to be in the hospital. Not having any idea how they would treat someone with those injuries, Molly had hit another wall. Maybe she would have to do some medical research, go to the hospital, and interview some nurses or interns to find out how they would actually treat a head wound.

She put the computer to sleep. Writing was supposed to be a way for her to relax. Doing research was work, so that was the end of that story. Maybe another plot would surface the next time her legs kept her awake at night.

Boredom brought an early bedtime. As she always did before going to bed, she rechecked all the locked doors. Even if she left the lights on, she doubted sleep would come. Tonight she had more than her damn legs to keep her awake.

Tired of sleeping on the recliner, she decided to try the bed. Bed was not a happy place. Bed was a place where her legs made her crazy. She sighed and crawled in. Maybe tonight would be different.

WHEN THE LIGHTED DIGITAL clock across the room declared it was 3:30 A.M., Molly's tingling legs woke her and demanded to be moved. Her eyes were wide open when she watched the clock change to 3:31 A.M. Suddenly, she stopped breathing. Something had come between her and the clock. She stifled a scream. Silence hung heavy; no movement, no noise, just the feeling of a presence in the room. The clock still showed 3:31 A.M. when it reappeared. Was her imagination playing tricks on her? Should she doubt her sanity?

Jumping out of bed, she raced around the house, turning on lights and checking all the locked doors that she had previously checked before going to bed. This was crazy! After the incident of the young drug runner who had entered her living area by crawling through an opening in the ceiling, she had called in a handyman who nailed the entrance shut. Just to be sure, she checked; the opening was secure.

Even though she was exhausted, sleep was out of the question. Mindlessly, she walked.

Chapter 31

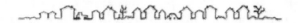

MORNING FOUND MOLLY asleep on the couch. She couldn't remember how she got there.

Today was closing day on Dr. Parker's Grass Lake house. Today she would send Clara her paycheck. Today she would pay the office bills that had piled up. Today, she assured herself, things would be better.

She flinched when reality hit and she had to admit she was kidding herself. Panicked over being locked in a pantry and scared because of a slashed tire, she knew it was going to take more than a paycheck to make things better.

She waited until the coffee had finished perking and the bread had popped up in the toaster before opening the front door, curious to see where her paper would be this morning. Because of a poor throwing arm, the previous paperboy had been replaced. There had been too many customer complaints about papers being launched onto roofs, embedded in shrubs, and sunk into water puddles. This morning she was pleased to see the paper had landed right by her door. Smiling at the improvement, she picked up the paper; her smile vanished. Looking back at her from the front page was another picture of Jerry Miller, as he would look today. Unlike the first picture that had been a local artist's rendition, this one had been computer generated.

She read the accompanying article while she ate. The murders at the Miller farmhouse had never been solved. Somewhere out there, still free, was Jerry Miller. The event at the farmhouse had opened up the cold case and the police were actively investigating again.

As she cleared the table, she took a long look at the picture. The first picture had been nonspecific; the computer-generated one fascinated her. Something about that face....

A glance at her watch told her she was running out of time. Not wanting to be late for the closing, she finished in the kitchen and headed for the shower.

The chosen suit was blue, the white blouse frilly, and the shoes sported high heels. Her red hair was caught back in a matching blue headband, and she adding small pearl earrings to finish the outfit. The magic of make-up hid the dark circles under her eyes.

Today's closing was at the title company's office. The entire Parker family smiled at her when she entered the room.

Immediately Molly's bad attitude about her choice of occupation changed. When she had buyers like the Parkers, it was easy to forget about the Lacys and the Blairs.

Since Miss Detail had taken care of all the obstacles, the closing ran smoothly. It ended with everyone complimenting each other on a job well done.

Dr. Parker noticed Molly's shaking hand when he gave her an envelope.

In answer to Molly's raised eyebrows, he smiled. "It won't bite you. It's an invitation to my open house!" There was concern on his face when he asked quietly, "Is everything okay?"

Molly flinched. She thought she was doing a good job of covering her feelings. "Thanks for asking. I didn't know it showed!" She tried to smile. "There are just some things happening in my life right now that are a bit upsetting."

"I know; I read about the farmhouse in the paper. That had to be a terrifying experience. I'm here if you want to talk about it."

Molly bit back a sob. "Thank you. I'll remember that offer." Regaining her composure, she said, "But back to your clinic, I was hoping you wouldn't forget about inviting me." She slit the envelope open and looked at the invitation. "I see it's this Friday night?"

"Yes. There's been a lot of advertising, so come early. I'd like to show you around personally before it gets crowded."

"I'll do that. And, I'd like to say to your entire family, welcome to the community!"

"Thank you, Miss Allen. You have been so very helpful. Finding the right house could have been a miserable job for all of us, but with your help, it has been quite pleasant."

Molly smiled. She loved a good ending.

FRIDAY NIGHT FOUND HER looking forward to the sleep clinic open house, if for nothing more than a welcome break.

Not knowing what people wore to sleep clinic open houses, she chose to go half-casual, half-dressy; no jeans, but no emerald green dress, either. A tailored pair of soft gray pants topped with a multi color silk blouse graced her small frame. She twisted her red hair up in a loose bun with tendrils falling around her face.

She smiled at her image in the mirror. Green eyes and dimples grinned back at her. If the best she could do for a Friday night date was a sleep clinic open house, so be it.

THE SLEEP CLINIC WAS FULL of people who, like Molly, were curious about the services such a clinic could provide. There were pamphlets to be picked up and literature to be read. The four clinic doctors circulated around welcoming people and answering questions.

She picked up a pamphlet titled: "You are not alone!" Not alone for what, she wondered? She read: "It's bedtime, and you want to go to sleep, but your legs won't let you."

"What?" she exclaimed loudly.

"What's that about 'what'?" asked a man's voice.

Molly looked up. A smiling Dr. Parker was standing beside her.

"What's this pamphlet about?"

"It's about a condition called Restless Legs," explained Dr. Parker.

"That condition has a name?" a stunned Molly asked.

"Yes. Restless Legs is a very common problem. Nearly one in ten adults has some form of it."

Molly's mouth dropped open. "Dr. Parker, I can't believe what you're telling me."

He looked at her strangely. "Of course you can believe me! Why? Is this a problem?"

She was having trouble breathing. "I have legs like that, and I was told that I needed to see a psychiatrist."

His forehead creased as he raised his black eyebrows. "You think you have restless legs?"

"Think?" she wailed, "I know! I've suffered all my life with weird sensations in my legs."

Dr. Parker, seeing how agitated she was, laid a hand on her shoulder. "Have you told your doctor about it?"

She willed herself to calm down. "I have to admit that I haven't since I moved here. Who would want to buy a house from a crazy agent? But I have told him that I can't sleep at night. The most I ever got was some sample pills to try."

"Did the sample pills work?"

Molly relaxed. "If walking into walls and falling off chairs count, they worked. But they did nothing to calm my legs. You know, I like the fact that now I have a name for my crazy legs."

"Not only do we now have a name for your crazy legs," grinned Dr. Parker, "we have medication for them!"

"This is almost too much for me to take in and believe," she said, shaking her head. "What do I do now? I can't believe there is help for something I've suffered with all my life."

"Well, the first thing you do is to consult a sleep doctor."

"I have the feeling that I already know one of those. Right?"

"You certainly do! Call my office in the morning. Here's one of my new cards, and you'll be my first patient," he said. "Now I'd better circulate and meet some of the people who were interested enough to come tonight."

Molly shook her head as Dr. Parker walked away. Talk about the fickle finger of fate! What were the chances that one of her buyers would have the solution to her leg problem? Restless Legs. What an appropriate name!

Chapter 32

THE LAST THING MITCH wanted to do on Saturday morning was to pick up the girls, but that was the agreement he had made with the Westins. Bone tired from a week in the field, he would have preferred a few more hours in bed. He'd spent most of the morning looking for his cell phone. He was almost positive he had left it on the bathroom counter, but his memory must be wrong because it sure wasn't there.

However, he knew Kim and Laurie would be anxiously waiting for him to pick them up. The week had to have been hard on the grandparents since this was their first attempt to spend time with May's children since the accident.

It had been a hard week for him, too. The fieldwork had been exhausting but Mitch now felt better prepared to handle his new promotion. He especially liked the days spent in the forest working with tracking dogs. It was good that the busy days had kept his mind off the 'Molly thing'.

At night, however, just about the time his eyes were closing, the picture of her sitting in that big chair would jar them open. Burned into his memory was the sight of her watching them through the window. His heart hurt every time he relived the moment when she had turned her face away from them. Sleep was hard to come by after that and most mornings found him grumpy and irritable.

Pulling into the Westins' driveway, he sat for a moment, his eyes closed, and his head bent. Sometimes the realization that he had the exclusive responsibility of taking care of Fred's two children overwhelmed him. At times, it felt almost like a physical blow. He was not sorry he'd accepted the task because he loved them and couldn't stand the thought of someone else doing it, but they sure did complicate his life.

The door of the house opened and Kim and Laurie ran out. He made it out of the car in time to open his arms for them.

"Does this mean you're glad to see your old Uncle Mitch?" he laughed as he swung both of the girls off their feet.

"Can we go home, can we, can we, please?" implored Kim.

The Westins hung back and smiled sheepishly.

"I don't think we did such a good job of keeping them busy," Grandma Westin said. "It has been so long since we had little ones in the house, I'm afraid we've gotten a little rusty."

"Girls, we promise it will be more fun next time," Grandpa Westin said, hugging Kim.

Laurie, feeling their discomfort, chimed in. "Grandma read us the best stories."

Getting into the spirit, Kim hugged her Grandpa back and said, "Grandpa gives us the best hugs!"

"See," said Mitch. "You haven't forgotten. You just need a little practice."

"Kim looks so much like our May did at her age." Grandma Westin's eyes filled with tears.

There was a moment of silence as everyone in the small group remembered the missing pieces, the pieces that had left such a huge hole in the lives of everyone standing there.

Mitch, his voice husky, broke the silence. "Go get your things, girls, and I'll take you home."

Toting their packs, the girls rushed out of the house, and, without a backward glance, yelled "Bye," and crawled into the car. Mitch looked at the grandparents and shrugged his shoulders as if to say, "Sorry about that."

The Westins nodded they understood and, hand in hand, they watched their beloved May's children leave.

"Mitch is a remarkable man," Mr. Westin said quietly.

When Mrs. Westin nodded, unchecked tears were running down her cheeks.

———————

THE GIRLS BOUNCED up and down in their seats, each one trying to yell over the other. Mitch was hearing two accounts of the past week's events. Each story was followed by an argument between the girls over which version was the correct one.

Mitch's head ached. Being stressed over his lost cell phone and the noise coming from the back seat pushed him over the edge. He snapped at them.

"Enough!"

A shocked silence followed.

With a sob Kim asked, "Don't you even want to know what we did with Grandma and Grandpa?"

"I'm sorry, girls," his voice broke. "I had a bad week."

"Ours wasn't so nice, either," Laurie muttered. "Grandma cried a lot."

Kim, her face puckered up, added, "And we didn't know what we did to make her cry, either!"

"We tried to be extra good, but sometimes that made her cry even harder." Laurie sounded near tears herself.

Mitch swallowed a sob. Grief never seems to have an end. Glancing into his rear-view mirror, his heart broke when he saw Laurie, tears running down her cheeks, comforting a sobbing Kim.

"Hey!" he said, feeling it was time to banish the blues, "how about visiting Grandma and Grandpa Hatch on the lake? Maybe Grandpa will take us all out in his pontoon boat!"

Kim gave one last sniff; Laurie blew her nose. Mitch could almost feel the girls' mood change.

He smiled; his plan had worked. The voices coming from the back seat sounded happy when they yelled, "Yeah, let's go to the lake!"

Chapter 33

MITCH'S PARENTS, MARILYN and Richard, lived on a beautiful little lake. The bottom of the spring-fed body of water was covered with clamshells that shimmered on sunny days.

No one answered the door when Mitch and the girls rang the bell.

"Oh, not again!" wailed Laurie.

"But the doorbell worked this time. I heard it," exclaimed Kim.

"Maybe they're in the back. Let's walk around the house to the lake side."

MARILYN AND RICHARD were down by the lake, about to step onto their pontoon boat. Marilyn's face broke into a big smile when she saw them rounding the house, heading for the lake.

"What a nice surprise!" she called to them.

Richard paused in his effort to start the boat and waved his hand. "Welcome aboard!"

Without protest, the girls wiggled into their life vests. They knew from previous trips on the pontoon that Grandpa Hatch wouldn't take them for a ride until they buckled up.

"Everybody ready?" Grandpa Hatch yelled over the noisy motor. "Then, off we go!"

The boat ride was peaceful, beautiful, and calming to Mitch. There is something about being around water on a sunny day that puts life's problems into perspective. He watched his parents, now in their mid seventies, beaming at their granddaughters. The girls were shouting the details of the week's visit with their other grandparents, but Marilyn and Richard were having trouble hearing over the noisy motor. Richard pulled the boat into a cove and shut it off. "Let's just sit here a bit and have a civilized conversation without yelling."

"Good idea," Marilyn agreed.

The silence was almost deafening. Two loons, along with their babies, swam past. One disappeared into the water, reappeared with a small fish, and fed one of the chicks.

"That must be the mother loon," decided Kim. "Mothers feed their babies.

The loon repeated the process, and to the little girl's dismay, gave the fish to the same baby. The other baby loon protested.

"What kind of a mother are you?" demanded Kim, shaking her finger at the bird.

With that, the birds moved rapidly away from the boat.

"Kim, don't worry. Loons are good parents; that other baby will get fed," Marilyn hugged her,

"Promise?" Kim's eyes were full of unshed tears.

In an effort to move past the loon incident, Richard pointed to the neighbor's house. "See that sold sign? Our neighbors sold their house last week."

"I didn't even know it was on the market," Mitch said. "Where are the Grays going?"

"They've had enough winters, they say, so they're moving to someplace warmer. I forget what state, though."

"I think Don said it was South Carolina," Marilyn said. "I saw the new owner and his kids down by the water. The kids were pushing each other off the dock."

"I heard that the new owner was some kind of sleep doctor," Richard added. "Doctors seem to be specializing in everything these days."

Mitch remembered Molly being excited about selling a lake house. He asked, "Did either of you get a glimpse of the agent?"

"I did," grinned Richard. "And she was a looker! A redheaded looker! I was surprised to see her picture in the paper the other day."

Mitch's quick intake of breath at the description of the agent didn't go unnoticed. Marilyn's antenna quivered; whatever was going on in Mitch's life, she was positive the redheaded agent was involved.

"What did she do to get her picture in the paper?" Mitch asked.

Marilyn detected an edge in her son's voice.

"You know the old farmhouse on Miller Road?"

Mitch nodded.

"Well, she thought she was showing the farm to a developer but turns out he wasn't one," Richard said.

"Well, if he wasn't a developer, who was he?"

"No one knows. He locked her in the pantry and left her there."

Marilyn saw a look of horror on her son's face.

"Left her there? For God's sake, Dad, finish the story! Did she get out?"

"Yes, she got out. She had her cell phone with her and called for help," Richard paused and then said thoughtfully, "I've got to get me one of those things! It would come in handy. I could call Marilyn to come and get me when my bike has a flat tire."

Marilyn rolled her eyes.

Mitch couldn't believe it. Dad thought Molly was all right, but was she? He'd get the full story tomorrow when he went back to work. It struck him that even out here on the lake he couldn't get rid of the 'Molly thing'. The sale of that lake house was one of the things they were going to celebrate the night she refused to answer the door.

He shook the thoughts out of his head.

"Hey, Dad, speaking of your bike rides, how many smashed helmets do you have lined up on the garage shelf now?"

Marilyn beat Richard to the answer. "Three. The latest one is from his smashing his head into that truck's cab!"

"Aw, Marilyn, cut it out. I've been teased enough about it!" Richard complained.

Marilyn wasn't finished. "Riding up the ramp of that truck is not the only time he rode with his head down!"

"For God's sake, Marilyn," Richard pleaded, "that's ancient history! Let sleeping dogs lie!"

"A sleeping dog, my foot, Richard," Marilyn laughed. "It's more like a dead deer!"

"A dead deer? Where's the dead deer? Can we see the dead deer?" clamored Kim.

"No, Kim, there's no dead deer to see," Mitch chuckled. "So, what's the story, Mom? Are you going to tell it, or is Dad?"

Richard muttered, "It's my story, so I guess I ought to tell it."

"Does this story start, 'Once upon a time'?" questioned Kim.

"No, it doesn't!" replied a grouchy Richard. "I was just trying to ride up that big hill on 669. So I put my head down so that I could pump hard to make it to the top of the hill when I …."

"Dad, I couldn't hear what you said at the end of that sentence. You were mumbling."

Marilyn was bent over laughing.

"Oh, all right. So I didn't see the dead deer on the road! What's the big deal, anyway? It had already been run over once, so I sure didn't hurt it running over it again!"

Now, everyone on the boat was laughing.

179

What a pleasant way to spend a Saturday afternoon, thought Mitch. If he could make a wish right now, it would be that the coming week would be as pleasant as this moment on the boat. He knew that the odds of that happening were zero to none. Work, his lost cell phone, and the 'Molly thing' would be waiting for him Monday morning.

A sense of urgency hit Mitch like a punch in the stomach. Monday morning was not good enough; he had to find Molly today. But how could he handle going into town while he still had the girls?

The pontoon boat ride over, Mitch sidled up to his mother on the way into the house. "Mom, I need a favor."

Marilyn stopped walking. "What kind of favor?"

"I need to go to the office and check my messages and my mail. I've been gone a whole week, so if you can come up with a reason for the girls to stay here with you for an hour or so, I'd love you forever!"

Marilyn knew it wasn't messages and mail that was giving her son so much angst; something else was going on. She looked back at her two granddaughters who were having a one-sided chat with their granddad. Richard was just listening and nodding his head. "Girls," she called, "I'm feeling like a picnic! Anyone else feeling like a picnic?"

Kim wrinkled her brow. "I don't know what a picnic feels like. Would I like to feel like a picnic?"

"If the picnic has hot dogs and s'mores," Laurie chimed in, "I'd feel like a picnic!"

"So be it, then," Marilyn laughed. "A picnic with hot dogs and s'mores it is!"

Mitch hugged his mom, kissed the top of her head, and headed for his car.

He had to see Molly! He had to look at her with his own two eyes to make sure she was all right. Maybe she didn't want to have a relationship with him; he could understand that. But couldn't he just be a friend? How could she object to that?

He pulled into a parking spot right outside Allen Real Estate. Looking through the window, he saw a dark office. There was a 'CLOSED' sign on the door. The office was closed? Obviously, everything wasn't all right with Molly. A call to her home produced nothing, not even an answering machine.

Anxiety was building inside him. He sat in his car and mulled over the problem. There should be a way to find out where she was. After all, wasn't he a detective?

The sound of his stomach growling reminded him that he hadn't eaten lunch. The sandwich shop was right down on the corner, and with a sigh, he opened the car door and got out; might as well solve the problem on a full stomach.

Entering the sandwich shop, he stopped in his tracks and sucked in his breath. The flash of Molly's red hair caught his eye, her laughing face made his heart beat faster, but the sight of a handsome man sharing her table sent a knife through his heart.

Mitch lost his appetite. He turned and walked out of the sandwich shop.

Chapter 34

SATURDAY MORNING MOLLY woke up wet with sweat and tangled in the sheets, struggling to extract herself from the paralyzing clutches of a nightmare. Knowing that dreams have a way of vanishing rapidly, she closed her eyes and willed herself to remember. Vague thoughts and feelings were all that came to mind, but she was sure a pitch-black pantry was in there somewhere.

Nobody should have to get out of bed this early in the morning, she thought, and then her face brightened; she really didn't have to. Nothing was going on at the office, Clara was with her grandkids, and there certainly was nothing happening in her social life.

Still half asleep, she curled herself into a ball and pulled the covers over her head. With the threat of a returning nightmare, did she even want to go back to sleep?

Last night! How could she have forgotten last night? Her head popped out from under the covers and her arm reached over to the nightstand where she'd put all the literature and brochures from the sleep clinic.

A leisurely morning like this called for breakfast in bed. She made her way to the kitchen, started coffee, and put bread into the toaster.

Soon, she was back in bed, breakfast tray on her lap, a cup of coffee in one hand and a brochure in the other. She choked on her first sip of coffee when she read, "discuss eliminating caffeine and alcohol with your doctor."

What? No coffee? Coffee was necessary! How do you start the day if you can't have coffee?

She delved into the next pamphlet. The first sentence refuted the diagnosis of all her old doctors: "Restless Legs Syndrome is a medical condition. It's not all in your head."

For some time Molly sat with that pamphlet in her hand, relishing her vindication. All her life she had shied away from situations that would reveal her problem. While in school, she had declined all sleepover invitations, on airlines, she always demanded an aisle seat, and in church or a theater, the back row was her choice. Outside her family, few people knew about her legs because she was determined that no one was going to call her crazy. Now she was holding proof in her hands that she could show to the world; her funny legs had nothing to do with her head. With a smile, she picked up another pamphlet.

One brochure even had a quiz to find out if you might have restless legs. *Yes*, she had a compelling urge to move her legs, *yes,* moving her legs relieved her symptoms, *yes*, her legs got worse when she was trying to rest, and *yes*, the urge to move got worse in the evenings.

Molly closed her eyes and laid back on her pillow. Her legs made internal demands that they be moved at night. But she had no bandages or scars to show the world in the morning; there were only dark circles and puffy eyes. No one could see her bone-tired body.

Monday morning she would call Dr. Parker and make an appointment. She put the coffee cup out of reach on the nightstand and ate her toast. If giving up coffee would make her nights easier, then coffee was history. What a relief to discover there was a name for her problem and medication to treat it.

With her breakfast tray safely on the nightstand, she snuggled back amid the scattered brochures and fell asleep.

Elation over finding a remedy for her damn legs put a smile on her face as she slept. No nightmare disturbed her dreams.

SUNSHINE COMING THROUGH the window woke Molly. Feeling lazy, she rolled over and looked at the clock. Noon! She had slept until noon! Scrambling out of bed, she knocked over the breakfast tray as she ran into the bathroom. A glimpse of her tousled hair in the mirror made her laugh. There were no signs of the guilt she could feel for sleeping until noon. Why should she feel guilty about sleeping? In fact, she was in the mood to continue this unplanned holiday from work; lunch at the sandwich shop would fit right into this day.

Showered and dressed, Molly picked up the morning paper from the porch as she left her house. Eating alone with nothing to read was always an uncomfortable thing for her; the paper would solve that problem.

Stepping into the sandwich shop, she observed the 'Seat yourself' sign, and headed for a vacant table in the back. She sat down and opened the paper. Looking up at her was a picture of a man holding a book. She proceeded to read the story about M. D. Penwell, a writer who was in town doing a book signing at the local library. Molly frowned. The book he was promoting, "Life Among the Angels", was not a new book; in fact, she had read it several years ago. Deep into reading the article, she was unaware that someone was standing by her table. A shuffle of feet got her attention and, looking up, she found herself gazing into the bluest eyes she had ever seen. She gasped.

"Sorry if I surprised you," the man said. "May I sit down?"

Startled by the request, Molly didn't answer.

"It's one of two things," the grinning man said as he pointed at the picture. "You either don't like my book or you don't like my picture. So which is it?"

She glanced at the paper, looked up at the man, and then down at the picture.

Laughing, the man said, "Yes, that's me! I confess!"

Pictures lie. The one in the paper didn't show the color of his thick mop of auburn hair, his sparkling blue eyes, his chiseled chin, his toned body, or the aura of pure sex that practically dripped from his six-foot frame. "May I sit down," he asked again.

Molly nodded. Nodding was easier than speaking.

"I should explain," M. D. Penwell said as he sat down. "You walked in just as I was asking the waitress who in town could help me find something to rent. I understand you are Miss Allen, owner of Allen Real Estate?"

Molly had regained her composure. She smiled and said, "Yes, I can, and yes, I am! But I want you to know that I only work with people who call me Molly."

"I can do that!" he smiled, "and please call me Dean."

Molly couldn't believe her luck. Sitting at her table was a writer who could actually finish a story.

"Tell you what," Molly proposed. "Since I've never known an honest-to-goodness published author, I'd like to just talk and have lunch with you."

"What about finding a rental for me?"

"Oh, we'll do that after lunch. Is that okay with you, Dean?"

He looked at her and grinned.

"Did I say something funny?" Molly asked.

"I'll bet that I'm looking at someone who is interested in writing and wants to pick my brain. How right am I?" he asked.

Molly blushed. "You're very right. Does this happen to you frequently?"

He thought for a moment. "Molly, the world is full of wannabe writers, but few ever follow up on their dream. And, if they do, they find that writing is hard...really hard. Most give up; only a very few stick to it."

Molly shook her head in agreement. "I'm one of those writers who can't stick to it. I try, but I always get to a point where I can't figure out what comes next."

Dean grinned. "That's not a good feeling, is it?"

"No, it sure isn't! You don't seem to have that problem. Your plots are always good. I like the books that you've written, especially the one you're promoting at the library."

Dean looked down at the table, and then raised his eyes. "Molly, I need you to find me a secluded lake cottage to rent for a few months." He played with the silverware, then picked up a spoon and waved it at her. "The reason I'm still promoting my old book is because I don't have a new one."

"So write one!" Molly exclaimed. "You published authors don't seem to have any trouble coming up with ideas for your next book."

He looked at her in disbelief. "Molly, I don't know where you got the idea that writing ever gets easy, because it doesn't! Just because I have had several books published doesn't mean I can do it again."

"But you write a good story!" she protested. "What's the problem?"

"The problem, Molly, is that I've been working on a story line for so long I'm sick of it. I've painted myself into a corner and I can't find a way out so," he leaned across the table, "I'm thinking new surroundings might help me. I need to come up with a twist in the plot that will get me out of that corner."

Molly looked at him in amazement. She was talking to a professional writer who had the same problems she had in finishing her stories. Molly wasn't expecting that answer.

She laughed.

She didn't see a startled Mitch turn and leave the sandwich shop.

Chapter 35

EVERY SUNDAY FOR THE LAST fifteen years, Allen Real Estate had held a house open to the public. If Molly really wanted to feel depressed, figuring out how many Sundays that would be would do it.

The listing she was holding open today was a 'spec' house constructed by a builder on the speculation that someone would buy it. This particular spec was a cute little starter home that should appeal to a large section of the buying public. Clara had put an ad in the weekend paper announcing that the house would be open Sunday from one to four.

She drove to the road at the intersection leading into the subdivision and stopped. In her trunk, she had a stack of open house signs. While she was putting out a sign, a late model car slowed down. The man driving the car caught Molly's eye and then drove on.

The same car drove slowly past her again while she was putting a sign at the next intersection. This time Molly tried to get a better look at the man, but a wide-brimmed hat kept his face in the shadows.

Molly knew the dangers involved in holding a house open. The signs she had just put up pointed to a house where the chances were good that a woman would be there alone.

As she walked toward the house, she pulled out her cell phone and called Clara.

"Hey, Girlfriend, it's good to hear from you. It would be even better if you assured me that I still have a job!'

"Never doubt that, Clara. I have to believe that business will pick up."

"I got the check from the Grass Lake closing. Thanks," Clara said. "Since this is Sunday, I suppose you're calling me to be your back-up. What's the code word today?"

Molly spoke slowly. "We joke about this, but I really might need you today. A man was following me around in his car while I was putting up signs."

"Maybe it's an interested buyer?"

"Could be, but it doesn't hurt to cover our bases."

"Right," Clara agreed. "It would help if I knew what house you're holding open."

"Remember that little starter home on your side of town?" Molly asked. "You put the ad in the paper... the one on Woodland Drive. I want you to call me every fifteen minutes. If everything is fine but I have a customer and can't talk, I'll say, "Want to have lunch next week?"

"Yes, I would."

"We sound like Abbot and Costello," Molly cackled. "I say 'Want to have lunch' if everything is fine."

"Got it, but why can't you just say 'everything's fine'?" Clara protested.

"It's a game!" laughed Molly.

"Well it wasn't a game at the farmhouse," Clara reminded her.

Molly was silent. "You're right. We'll keep this serious. If everything is fine, I'll just say it's fine."

"I hear you," Clara said. "Now the biggie. What do you say if it's not fine?"

"If something bad is happening and I can't talk about it, I'll say, 'Lunch has been canceled'. Got it?"

"You know we do this silly code thing every Sunday, and it's mostly to amuse ourselves," Clara observed.

"I know," Molly agreed.

189

Clara chuckled. "When you were locked in the pantry and really needed to use the code word of the day which, I believe, was 'excellent', all you kept yelling was 'Oh my God!' Maybe we should just make that our permanent code."

Molly sucked in her breath in disbelief. "I can't believe you're teasing me about that awful experience!"

Clara was quiet for a moment. "I didn't mean to tease, believe me. That was a terrible thing that happened to you. Every day, even when I'm talking to you, I watch your face shut down and I know your mind has taken you back to that dark pantry. You don't talk about it, Molly. You need to talk about it."

"I'm not ready to talk about it!" Molly's voice was firm. "Are you a psychiatrist now?"

Clara sighed. "No, just a concerned friend." After a pause, she added, "I've got the code and I'll call 911 if you need help."

"Glad we got that straightened out," Molly said, relief in her voice, "because I won't say the code words unless I need to."

"Got it," Clara assured her. "I'll keep my cell phone with me until four o'clock. Hannah and Emma have about worn me out, so I think they need a nap this afternoon."

"I'll bet if you're cold you make them put on sweaters, too," Molly teased. "Have you just about gotten your fill of being a grandmother?"

"The girls go back to school tomorrow, so I'm off the hook after today. Jill took advantage of the fact that I'm still here and she's at the mall shopping. Should I show up at the office tomorrow morning?"

"I'll see you at nine tomorrow morning. Oh, I think someone is coming to the door. Talk to you later, bye."

Molly drew a sharp breath when she saw it was the man in the wide-brimmed hat. She was slow to register the fact that he was carrying her open house signs until he dropped them. Her first reaction to the clanking sounds when they hit the floor was confusion. Why would someone remove her signs? An irate property owner on whose lawn she had placed them? Puzzled, she opened her mouth to demand an explanation when reality hit. By removing the signs, the man had effectively shut down her open house. She knew with growing dread that no one else would be coming through the door; whoever this man was, she was on her own. Clara was supposed to call her every fifteen minutes, but since she had just hung up, it could be a very long fifteen minutes until she called again.

The man stood silent, his icy blue eyes never leaving her face. With trepidation, Molly watched him slowly remove his hat. A long ponytail, brown with streaks of gray, hung down his back and an unkempt, dark beard covered most of his face. His clothes were wrinkled and there was an unwashed smell about him.

Her first reaction, slamming the door, was futile; he easily pushed the door and stepped inside. Molly screamed. Running from him, she pulled the cell phone from her pocket.

"You don't want to do that, Mol," he said quietly. "Please put it away."

Molly froze. That voice!

"What?" The hair on her arms bristled.

"You heard me the first time, Mol. Put down that phone."

It was the voice in the loop that had been running round and round in her head for three years. How could this be? How could that voice be coming from this man? Only two people in this world called her Mol. One was her brother and the other one was…

"Dave?" She struggled to get the word past her constricted throat.

"Hello, Mol." He reached out and touched her face. She flinched.

"What's the matter?" he asked in a warm voice. "You don't seem pleased to see me!"

The shock of hearing Dave's voice stunned her. Old emotions were colliding with reality and, for a moment in Molly's head, the pain of the past three years disappeared in a flood of remembered love. But the man standing in front of her didn't look like Dave. How could this be? "I don't understand," her voice quivered. "Why are you here?"

His right eye twitched as he leaned toward her. "You mean besides getting to see you again? I've dreamed of this day for the past three years. Haven't you?"

Struggling to breathe, her teeth chattering, she shook her head. "Dream? How can I dream about someone I've never seen before? No, no, please, just go. Please!"

"I'm not leaving. Not until we settle a few things."

"Settle a few things? What things? You removed my signs, you've isolated me, and you're scaring me! Whatever it is you think we have to settle…forget it! I don't want to talk about it! Please, just go!" she begged.

His face changed; gone was the friendly smile. "Why are you making me repeat myself? I'm not leaving. No one will be coming to your rescue. I've seen to that." He pointed to the signs and then looked intensely into her eyes. "I've waited a long time for this moment."

"But you can't be Dave," she cried. "I've never seen you before in my life!"

He laughed. "Well, you almost did at the farmhouse."

She gasped. "That was *you*? *You* pushed me into that pantry?"

"I really hadn't planned on doing that, Mol, believe me." His eye twitched. "Sometimes I do things…," his voice trailed off.

Molly could feel panic building inside her. "Why?" she cried. "Why did you pretend to be a developer? Why did you lure me to the Miller farmhouse?"

"Because that's my house," he replied quietly.

"Your house? My God!" she peered at his face. It didn't look anything like the computer-generated picture in the paper. "You are...are you Jerry Miller?"

"That's my Mol! Always quick to figure out a puzzle. But you never figured me out, did you?" He laughed but there was little mirth in the sound. "Colored contacts, a change of hair color and style isn't exactly rocket science!"

Bile was rising in her throat. She swallowed hard. "How can you be Jerry Miller but sound just like Dave."

"Pretty clever of me, wouldn't you say?"

She shook her head in disbelief. "Are you going to tell me that you are both Dave and Jerry Miller?"

"Afraid you're going to hear something you won't be able to live with?" he cackled. "Afraid you're going to find out that you once loved a murderer?" He reached out his hand. "Yes, Mol, Dave and Jerry Miller are one and the same."

Molly jerked away, appalled. "Then I have no idea why you're here! Why would you even think I'd want to see either of you? Dave deceived me and Jerry Miller locked me in the pantry. I'm surprised you have the nerve to show your face!"

He threw his head back and laughed. The laughter stopped abruptly. His expression changed. "I'm here to talk about us."

Molly snorted. "Us? There is no 'us'!"

"But there was an 'us'!"

"I thought there was," Molly admitted. "For the past three years I've dreamed of having the chance to face you and tell you what your lies did to me!" Molly's eyes filled with tears.

"There was an 'us'!" he repeated, "but you wrecked it!"

Molly's mouth dropped open in surprise. "I wrecked it?

"You wrecked it! Yes, you did." Tears were running into his beard. "You just sat there in that stupid green dress and watched!" His face rapidly switched from sadness to anger. "The image of you in that green dress has haunted my dreams, awake or asleep. I curse that green dress!"

Molly choked back a gasp. There really was a curse on that green dress!

How many minutes before Clara's call? She gestured with her arms, glanced at her watch and babbled, "You didn't like my green dress? Why didn't you like my dress? You said you did." Ten more minutes.

"Don't change the subject, Mol," he warned, his eyes glaring at her.

"Dave, do you really think I should have followed you and the police out the door? To do what?"

"I was all alone!" he cried, his eyes blazing. "No one stepped in to help me. You're just like all the rest of them. You said you loved me, but you lied!"

Molly bristled. "Now, are you going to say that it was my fault you were already married? That was a low thing that you did to your wife, and let's not forget your kids and your business partner!" She stepped forward and raised her voice. "Now would you like to talk about what you did to *me*?"

"Bitch!"

The hand that slapped her across the face appeared so quickly Molly had no chance to move out of range. Her head snapped back and blood gushed from her nose. "You made me do that, Mol!" he cried as he pulled her to his chest.

Molly struggled to pull away. "Bitch? You called me a bitch?" she cried. "After what you did to me, how dare you show up out of the blue and call me names!"

"Show up out of the blue! That's rich, but then you old-maid school teachers are good with words!" he sneered. "I didn't show up out of the blue. All those years in the institution I dreamed and planned for this day!"

Molly's head jerked. Institution? Dave/Jerry spent time in an institution? New fear gripped her; she was isolated with an unstable man and no one was going to rescue her.

"Your picture is in the paper, Jerry or Dave, whoever you are, and the police are looking for you. What is so important that you would risk being captured? What are you doing here?"

"Payback time, Mol."

His arms were still tightly wrapped around her and her face was pinned to his chest. Blinding fear and panic were rapidly building inside her. Her mouth was dry, her heart was pounding, and a paralyzing feeling of utter helplessness swept over her. "You're scaring me!"

"Yeah, I'm scaring you. You were scared in the pantry, too. You didn't like the pantry, eh? I didn't either when my mom put me in there. Did you see the messages I carved in the wall?" His face contorted in the middle of a laugh.

In a flat voice he said, "What I'm going to tell you is funny, Mol, but if you laugh, I might just have to kill you."

He released her so suddenly she slid to the floor. Looking down at her, he added, "And then again, I might kill you even if you don't laugh."

"Kill me?" She was so stunned her tongue didn't want to move.

"Yes, kill you."

"Uh, 'kill you' as in making me dead, or 'kill you' as in a figure of speech?" She was amazed that her brain was still working.

"The first one, Mol."

"But why?" she gasped as she pulled herself to her feet.

"To get even."

"Get even for what?" She struggled for breath. "Help me understand!"

His hand came up, poised to strike her again; she flinched. "Aren't you even curious why I kil...why I did what I did to my family?" he asked as he stepped back.

"All right, I'll ask you," she replied in a subdued voice. "Why did you kill your family?"

He flinched as if it stunned him to hear those words come out of Molly's mouth.

"Well," Molly asked, "are you going to tell me?"

He couldn't look at her. "They were going to send me away," he said quietly.

"Away where?" Molly asked.

"To an institution; they said I was crazy."

In a pleading voice he asked, "Don't you see why I have to get even with you? I did an awful thing to my family so they couldn't send me away, and then you turned around and sent me there all on your own." With a sob in his voice, he cried, "It's like I kil...it's like I got rid of my family for nothing."

"Wait a minute!" she held up both hands in dismay. "I didn't send you anywhere! Please, Dave," she implored. "If you came back to punish me for something I did, I'd like to know what it is."

Dave looked at her, his face contorted. "After I..." he swallowed, "after I did that bad thing, I ran away to Detroit. I knew I had to invent a new me; not a crazy me, but a sane me. And I did. New name, new look...oh, you'll love this! In Detroit, I was a redhead with green eyes, just like you! Good thing I changed that when I came here, eh? I doubt you'd have been attracted to someone who looked like your brother."

He waited for her reaction, expecting at least a smile. When her expression didn't change, his lips curled and he jeered, "You didn't think that was funny, Mol? You used to laugh when I told you things. Were you just playacting the whole time, just weaving your web a little tighter around me?"

Molly wiped her bloody nose with her sleeve. "Have you forgotten? You said if I laughed, you were going to kill me. What you said wasn't funny enough to die for."

He blinked rapidly and regained his composure. "In Detroit I became a businessman, had a family, and all was well for a number of years. But my wife nagged and I didn't like my bratty kids, so I embezzled the money and fled before I did something bad to them. I came here and invented Dave. Remember sane Dave, Mol?" he asked. "I came back to my hometown...and met you."

Both of them were silent, remembering. Dave continued. "I never felt love before I met you. Life on the farm was hard. Dad was a mean drunk and my mom heard voices. I'm not making excuses for what I did to them, but there was no love in my life until I met you."

"And that's the reason you came back to get some kind of revenge?" she asked, disbelief in her voice. "So what did I do wrong?"

"You made me love you. That's what you did wrong!" he said in a soft voice.

"I'm not getting it, Dave. Love is a gift. You can't make someone love you."

"I don't know how you did it, but you did. Before my partner dropped the charges, I went to jail for embezzling. That's when I missed you so much I went out of my head!"

His eyes filled up with tears. "Missing you made me crazy. Really crazy. Years ago I..I did bad things to my family because they were going to put me in an institution. But you," he sobbed, "you put me there with so little effort."

His face softened and for a moment, his eyes filled with tenderness. "Can't you see? I don't want to kill you, but if I let you live, then it's like I kil...it's like what I did to my family was for nothing."

Anger over-powered her fear. "Loving me made this happen? You came back to punish me because you loved me? If that makes sense to you, then you *are* crazy!" Too late, she realized she had said the wrong word.

He whirled on her. "I knew it!"

With that, he pulled out a gun and aimed it at her head.

Molly's cell phone rang.

"No you don't," he yelled. "Not again! I let you get away with that at the farmhouse, but not here!"

Her vision tunneled and all she could see was the gun. Realizing that this was probably the last chance she would have to save herself, she took a deep breath, looked him in the eye, and said, "It's just my secretary! She's on her way here with lunch. If I don't answer it, she'll think I'm tied up with a customer and can't talk, and she'll just show up. Please let me tell her that I can't do lunch. You have no argument with her, so why would you want someone else to get mixed up in this mess? I promise, all I'll say is 'Lunch has been canceled'. Please!"

Dave pondered. The phone continued to ring.

"All right," he reluctantly agreed. "Answer it, but if you say more than 'Lunch has been canceled', I'm pulling the trigger and your secretary can listen to you die."

Molly answered her phone and said as clearly as she could, "Clara, lunch has been canceled." Looking him in the eye, she ended the call.

He grabbed the phone out of her hand, threw it across the room, and fired the gun.

The sight of Molly crumpled at his feet brought him a moment of sanity. Realizing what he had just done, he howled like an animal and ran out the door.

MOLLY MISSED SEEING the rescue party that crashed through the door. The bullet that whizzed past her ear and smashed into the wall so terrified her, she had passed out.

There were voices in the background, something wet was on her forehead and out of the fog, a familiar face was taking shape.

Tom! What was Tom doing here, sitting on the floor beside her? And why was he dressed in a police uniform? I'm not ready to wake up, she thought, and closed her eyes again.

"Molly, Molly, wake up!"

She opened her eyes. Tom was still there so she closed them again.

"Enough of this, Sis, wake up!"

Sis? So it was Tom.

Molly opened her eyes and gasped. The house was full of police officers, one of which was her brother.

"Am I dead?" she groaned.

"No, not dead, Mol! Thank God!"

"What happened?" she asked, holding her spinning head. "My ears are ringing and I'm covered with blood. Did he shoot me?"

"Looks like that blood is from your nose," Tom answered, "but when I ran through the door and saw you crumbled on the floor covered in blood,..." The catch in his voice told Molly everything she needed to know.

"And why are you dressed like that?"

"Gee, thanks!" he said as he hugged her. "Is that all you can say to your own brother who just rescued you?"

"But you're dressed like a cop! How can you be a cop?"

He grinned at her. "Big sisters don't know everything!"

Molly shook her head, unable to make sense out of what was happening. "This is too much," she said, while trying to get to her feet. "What happened here?"

Tom offered his hand. "That's what you're going to tell us, Mol," he said as he pulled her up. "When 911 called, I happened to be the closest patrol car."

Molly looked at her brother in disbelief. "You really are a policeman, then? You aren't just dressed for a costume party?"

Tom laughed. "You'll get used to the idea."

"If this is a joke, Tom…" She stopped when she saw the serious expression on his face; it was true. She shook her head and looked cautiously around the room. "Where is he?" she asked.

"If you're talking about the man we have in custody, he's at the station. When I turned onto this street and saw a car pull out of the driveway, I called for backup. Boy, was I scared! I was afraid of what I would find when I got here!" Tom paused long enough to hug his sister. "The guy didn't get very far, and they told me he didn't put up much of a fight. Molly, who is this guy? Do you know him?"

"Yes, I know him, and you do, too! We know him as Dave!"

"What do you mean, 'know him *as* Dave'? You mean he isn't Dave?"

"You'd better hope your backup men recognize who they have at the station! The man we knew as Dave is really Jerry Miller, the son who killed his family in that farmhouse on Miller Road."

Tom paused a moment to stare at Molly in shock, then whipped out his cell phone and called in the information. He ended the conversation by saying, "I'm bringing Molly to the station to make a statement, and no, I won't forget to ask her about the keys."

"What keys?" Molly asked.

"They found two sets of keys in his pocket. One of the sets had your office and house keys on it."

"How can they know that? Keys don't talk!"

"Remember those key chains you had made with the name of Allen Real Estate on them?" Tom asked.

Molly hit her forehead with the palm of her hand. "Of course! That explains it, and here I thought I was losing my mind!"

"What in the world are you talking about?" Tom demanded.

Molly's description of the clock that had disappeared for a second made Tom catch his breath. "That creep kept one of your house keys! He was in your house, watching you sleep? Now that's scary!"

Molly shook her head. "He didn't have to keep my key all these years. He just had to remember that fake rock I hide a spare key under. Guess that's not the smartest thing in the world to do," her smile revealed a hint of chagrin. "But now, about the other set of keys, I'll bet those are the keys to the farmhouse; tell your buddies at the station to work on that angle. The house hadn't been broken into, so I'm thinking Jerry kept the key when he left or maybe there was one hidden under a rock nearby. I'm not the only dumb person in the world who does that, you know."

Tom gave her an affectionate punch on the arm. "Now that we've got the key puzzle figured out, I have a few questions. How did Jerry Miller turn into the man we know as Dave? I'm a good judge of character and I thought the guy you were engaged to was great...until the police dragged him away!"

"Jerry Miller must have been a troubled boy because his mother punished him by locking him in the pantry. He got it into his head that they were going to send him away to an institution, so he killed all of them. The institution was Jerry's biggest fear; becoming a sane man was Jerry's ticket to avoid being sent there."

"When did it go wrong?" asked Tom.

"Wanting to get out of the family life he had created in Detroit, he embezzled money and headed back here." Molly stopped talking.

"That's where you entered the story, right?" Tom asked quietly.

Molly nodded. "I can't believe I was so gullible."

"Don't be hard on yourself, Mol, we all liked him, even Mom. She actually cooked for him, remember? So what happened?"

"Dave did the unthinkable and fell in love with me. When he was dragged away from me, he grieved over losing me, flipped, and was institutionalized. His worst nightmare happened because of me."

"I get it why Jerry was angry enough to kill you, but what beef did Dave have with you? What's his story?"

"Dave thought that by not defending him I had deserted him in his hour of need. Like I could convince the police not to take off with my fiancé? I don't think so!"

Molly sighed, stretched, and yawned. "I'm exhausted. Look at the hole in the wall! I have to call the builder and explain why he has to come back and fix the bullet damage. He's going to love that!"

"Mol, who owns this house?" asked Tom.

"This is a spec home; the builder owns it."

"After we get this all cleared up, I'd like to look more closely at this house."

"For what reason?" Molly asked, surprised.

"I've been thinking about buying," Tom said, looking around. "Something this size would be right up my alley."

Molly almost laughed. "I can't believe this. I might sell my brother the house I almost was killed in! Let me lock up so we can go to the police station. I want to give my statement and then go home. What an afternoon this has been!"

With all the questions answered at the station, a subdued Molly headed for home.

MOLLY'S CELL PHONE RANG as she pulled into her driveway. When she saw it was Clara calling, she quickly opened the phone and burst into tears.

"Molly, are you all right?" Clara cried.

"Oh, Clara. What would I do without you?" Molly cried.

Clara sobbed, "I've been waiting by the phone, scared to death, imagining all kinds of things happening to you!"

"I'm so sorry!" Molly lamented. "I should have called you right away, but with all the confusion…"

"You're forgiven. But what happened to you? I don't know anything! I've been going crazy."

Molly filled Clara in on the gory details and ended the story with a flourish. "I woke up to the strangest sight. My brother Tom responded to your call! He's a policeman and I didn't know it."

"Big sisters don't know everything."

"That's what he said." Molly paused and asked suspiciously, "You two in cahoots?"

"No," Clara answered slowly. "But maybe I'd like to be. Just how old is your brother, anyway?"

"Not old enough for the likes of you!" Molly teased.

"Oh, well," Clara sighed. "Hope springs eternal." There was a pause and then Clara said. "That's a pretty good system that we've worked out, Molly."

"Oh, by the way, why were you calling back so soon? I said to call every fifteen minutes, but thank God you called early."

"I forgot to ask you about Mitch. I wanted to know if you'd heard from him. He has to be back now if his phone message said he'd be back to work on Monday."

"The answer to that is no. And I don't really expect to hear from him."

"Then you have to call him, Molly. He has to hear your side of the story."

Molly answered sadly, "I have called him. He mustn't have liked the messages I left, because he hasn't called back."

"But you have to talk to him. He needs to know about your vampire legs. You sleep during the day because you can't sleep at night."

There was anguish in Molly's voice. "How can I tell him anything when he won't return my calls?"

"Molly, I'm so sorry. I was hoping you had good things to tell me."

"Oh, that reminds me. I do have something good to tell you. I might just get rid of my vampire legs, as you call them!"

"What are you planning to do," Clara snickered," cut them off?"

"Believe me, there have been some nights when I might have considered that! Remember I told you I had an invitation to Dr. Parker's open house?"

"Yes. The sleep clinic, right?"

"Right. Seems there is a name for what my legs do at night. The condition is called 'Restless Legs', and now they have medication for it! Pills that work! At least that's what Dr. Parker told me. I'm going to make an appointment to see him as soon as he can work me in."

"How about that," mused Clara. "You sell a house to a doctor who can solve your leg problem."

"Well, I'm hoping he can. And, that isn't the only good news. My knight-in-shining-armor brother liked the house I was holding open, and he's thinking about buying it."

Clara let out a short laugh. "If there is ever a prize for the craziest and scariest open house ever, I think the one you had today would win."

Chapter 36

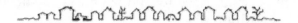

AT SIX-THIRTY MONDAY morning, Tom arrived at the parking lot with a bag slung over his shoulder and a cup of coffee in his hand. The bus that was to take the second week's bunch to training was already half full.

The driver was not on the bus. Tom looked around, finally spotting him talking on his cell phone some distance away. He couldn't hear what the driver was saying, but if waving arms and shrugging shoulders were any indication, something was wrong.

Latecomers running toward the bus slowed down when they saw there was no danger of being left behind.

The quiet of the morning was broken by the arrival of a very noisy tow truck. Jumping out of the truck, the driver added his own waving arms and shoulder shrugging to that of the bus driver. Some of the bus occupants got off to see what was going on.

Ending the conversation with a flurry of arms and head shaking, the bus driver walked back to the waiting group. "Seems like we have a problem with this here bus," he told them. "Can't be fixed, so it's gonna be towed back to the barn. Another bus will be here shortly."

A groan went up from the captive audience.

"Won't be but a minute," assured the driver.

WANTING TO GET TO WORK a bit early his first day back on the job, Mitch was surprised to find people with suitcases milling around in the parking lot.

"Hey Mitch!" one of his fellow detectives yelled as Mitch approached the group. "Did you see another bus coming this way?"

Mitch laughed. "What do you mean, 'another bus'? How many do you need?"

"Just one that works!" the co-worker joked.

Tom, who had been listening to the exchange, looked with interest at the man who had identified himself as Mitch. Were Detective Hatch and Mitch one and the same?

He walked up to Mitch, held out his hand. "Detective Hatch, remember me? I'm Tom Allen, your undercover man in the drug murders."

"So that was you!" Mitch grabbed Tom's hand. "I never really got to see your face, you know."

"I didn't want anyone to see my face. Sammy would have made short work of me if he even had a hint!"

"Did you know that was my first case?" Mitch was excited finely to meet his informant. "I want to thank you."

"Just doing my job, but thanks," Tom said graciously. Then in a more serious voice, he continued. "Now to change the subject, I believe you know my sister."

"Your sister?" Mitch had a blank look on his face. "Who would that be?"

"Molly Allen."

Mitch, his mouth open in surprise, stared at Tom. So that was it all along. Why hadn't he noticed? Tom and Molly looked alike. All that red hair, the green eyes, and Tom even had a dimple in one cheek. Mitch was pretty sure Molly had dimples in both cheeks, but he would check that the next time he saw her.

That thought stopped him short. There wasn't going to be a next time; Molly had seen to that. Mitch hastened to ask, "No, I had no idea she was your sister. But is she all right? I heard about her bad experience at an old farmhouse."

"She's still pretty shook up about it, but that was a minor thing compared to what happened to her at Sunday's open house!"

Mitch's heart lurched. Something bad had happened to Molly? The noise of the approaching bus injected a sense of urgency into the conversation.

"Mitch, I think there's a problem between you and my sister that could be easily solved. You should call her."

Mitch's mind was reeling with images of Molly. What kind of bad thing had happened to her? Realizing that Tom was waiting for a reply, he frowned in annoyance and said, "I don't see that happening!"

"Believe me, she's very upset about what happened."

"She's upset? That's hard to believe!"

"Call her and let her explain. Please."

"Sounds like you know more about me and Molly than I do." To Mitch's surprise, just saying their names together sent a little pang through his heart. Something bad had happened to Molly?

Tom paused, wondering if that fleeting expression on Mitch's face meant anything. "Yes, I do. We had lunch together at Mother's, and Molly told us what happened."

Mitch snorted. "Did she have a good laugh while she told you?"

"Laugh?" Tom raised his red eyebrows. "Mitch, she cried! Call her and let her explain."

"I can't imagine how she plans to explain how she watched us pound on the door," Mitch said, remembering the scene. "She never even got up from her chair."

The bus was pulling into the lot so Tom spoke quickly. "That's because she was asleep."

Mitch made a strangling sound that turned into a bitter laugh. "Asleep?"

"Molly has always had a problem sleeping at night," Tom explained hurriedly. "That's why she was walking the night of the double murders."

"Did you make up this excuse, or did she?" Mitch was angry. Poking Tom in the chest with his finger, he yelled over the noisy bus, "Did she put you up to this?"

The bus was quickly filling with disgruntled people who had waited two hours for a bus that was promised by the driver, 'It won't be but a minute!'

"Honest, Detective Hatch, Molly feels awful. Give her another chance!"

With that, Tom climbed onto the bus, found a seat, and watched out the window as Mitch, his head down, walked toward the office.

MITCH WAS DEEP in thought about his conversation with Molly's brother. Could there be such a simple answer to the incident that was eating his heart and stealing his sleep? He walked past Captain Hilburn's office, stopped, and retraced his steps. It was such an unusual sight to see his commander with his head down on the desk that Mitch risked being out of order and stepped into the room.

"Everything all right, sir?"

The captain's red face, when he raised his head, was full of suppressed anger. "Some people count to ten before they explode," he explained with clenched teeth, "Me, I take a moment to gather more strength so that when I do explode, things happen. Hatch, heads are going to fly!"

When Mitch unconsciously touched his neck, the captain said gruffly, "Not your head, Detective!"

Mitch relaxed. "Then who is going to be headless when whatever is bothering you is over?"

"The whole damn evidence department! They screwed up the electronic messages that put Sammy the Grunt and his two buddies in jail for the McGuire murders."

"Wait a minute!" Mitch cried. "That can't be! We have the pictures to prove he killed both those guys! How could that be screwed up?"

"Go ask the damn evidence department!" Regaining his composure, he added, "I don't have all the details, and I don't know what finally removed the charges against them. All I do know is those pictures have been thrown out. Sammy got himself a real shyster of a lawyer who, among other things, proved he could change a picture into anything he wanted by using a simple downloaded computer program. He made quite a sensation when he showed how easy it was to change the faces on the pictures. The judge and two federal agents weren't too happy when the finished photos placed all three of them at the murder scene. In addition, since the pictures were sent over the Internet, he questioned the chain of evidence. Their lawyer even found a few more loopholes that we've yet to hear about."

"So why are you beheading your own departments when it appears we were all outsmarted by a sharp lawyer?" Mitch asked, and then bit his tongue.

Captain Hilburn glared at Mitch, opened his mouth to remind him who he was talking to, and then changed his mind. "I guess I should thank you for stopping me before I did something I'd regret later. The thought of Sammy the Grunt being free just absolutely enrages me, but it looks like it's going to happen."

"I thought we had a tight case." Mitch shook his head. "So, Sammy the Grunt is going to be running around free as a bird. Now that's a frightening thought! Wonder where he'll go?"

"Anywhere but back here," said the captain. "He wouldn't dare come back here, because we know what he looks like!"

"Do we know much about those other two who went to jail with him?"

"Not really. According to Tom, Sammy had them off running errands. I probably wouldn't recognize those two because the Feds whisked them away pretty fast, but Sammy I would! He's a dirty-mean-vicious-ugly-scraggy-tall-skinny-long-grayhaired-slime-ball-son-of-a-bitch...with rotted teeth."

Mitch snorted. "That's quite a description! I hope you never have the occasion to describe me."

The captain chuckled, "Keep your nose clean, Hatch, and I'll never have to!"

Chapter 37

THE EXERCISE HOUR in the prison's courtyard was about to end. Prisoners were already lining up, waiting for the guards to escort them back to their cells. A side door opened, an inmate stepped out and stood quietly scanning the group. A startling white smile of recognition lit up his face.

Albert and Clarence, huddling together at the back of the line, were engaged in quiet conversation. "Buck up," Albert whispered in Clarence's ear.

"Buck up? Is that all you can say?" Clarence sobbed, using his sleeve to wipe the blood dripping from his nose.

Their conversation stopped abruptly when the new arrival stepped up to them, flashed them a smile, and said, "Well, Albert and Clarence! Imagine meeting you here!"

Not recognizing the man, Clarence and Albert edged closer to each other.

"You don't recognize me?" the man teased, pleased that indeed they didn't.

Albert's head shot up. The voice. "Sammy?" he whispered.

Sammy threw back his head and laughed, displaying a mouth full of black and white teeth. "The one and only!"

"But what have you done?" stammered Clarence.

With much glee, Sammy entertained them with stories about how he had snitched on his fellow cellmates and gained entrance into the guard's exercise room. Rolling up his sleeve, he proudly showed the beginnings of a muscle. And his teeth? A social worker had convinced the board that Sammy's life of crime was caused by black teeth that had given him an inferiority complex. New dental techniques that were destined for Hollywood were being used on Sammy. Eventually, all his teeth would be brilliantly white.

"Oh, I must congratulate you on your new short and cute hairstyle," Albert commented sweetly. "What did your hairdresser call that color, Sammy? Summer Gold? It does *so* bring out the blue in your eyes."

Sammy's fist came up fast, hesitated, and then went back down. He wasn't about to get into a situation where Albert's fist might ruin his new smile.

Albert snorted. "And I've seen girls with bigger muscles."

Sammy bit his tongue; his fist ached to punch Albert. He took deep breaths. He was having a hard time keeping his aggression in check. There was more than just teeth to protect; he didn't want to mess up all the good work his lawyer had put into his case. "Albert, you have something you want to say to me? Seems like you aren't that glad to see me," Sammy challenged.

Word had spread through the prison that Sammy had hired a lawyer. Details had a way of being distorted when passed from cell to cell, and prisoner to prisoner. Albert, hearing the gossip, figured that Sammy had found a way to end his prison sentence but hadn't included the two of them.

"So tell me, Sammy, how did you do it?" Albert demanded.

"Do what?" Sammy asked innocently.

"How did you get the lawyer, where did you get the money to pay the lawyer, and here's the big one," Albert almost shouted as he grabbed Sammy's collar, "why aren't Clarence and me gettin' out, too? You were the one with the fast knife!"

Sammy looked around wildly. All he needed was one bad report and it was all over. "No, no, Albert! You have it all wrong!" He tried to pull away. "I'm getting' out first, but you two won't be long behind me. That's what I came to tell you! Now get your hands off me!"

Albert dropped his hands. "So talk," he said.

As a token of appreciation for a dirty job well done, a fellow inmate had given Sammy the name of a lawyer. Sammy had left out that sordid little detail as he explained the rest. Their case had been unusual and his lawyer, who Sammy was paying out of their buried box, had found a loophole.

Clarence couldn't believe what he was hearing. "Say 'Honest to God' and cross your heart," he pleaded.

Sammy looked solemnly at Clarence, crossed his heart, and repeated the requested words. "When's it gonna happen?" Clarence asked. "I gotta get out of here!"

Sammy sneered and pointed at Clarence's still dripping nose. "The big boys pickin' on you, are they?"

Clarence hung his head.

"The big boys would have played a lot harder with you if I hadn't put the word out!" Sammy bragged. "Didn't you ever wonder why all of a sudden they let up a bit on you? That's because I told them to lighten up."

Clarence's face clouded. He looked at Albert and mouthed the words, "Then it wasn't Jesus?" Albert suppressed a smile and shook his head. Sammy had just solved the puzzle of why the bullying had mostly stopped.

"This gettin' out is gonna take months before anythin' happens," Sammy said. "But it's gonna happen."

"Months?" Clarence moaned.

"Are you stupid, boy?" Sammy chided. "We're talkin' months, not years!"

Albert's head was spinning with this new information. The prison sentence the three of them had gotten was so severe he had lost all hope. His life, which had started out with so much promise, was over. The thought that he might have a second chance was humbling.

Albert asked Sammy, "Where you gonna go when you get out?"

Sammy smile was malevolent. "First, I have to pay our lawyer, so I'm goin' back to that godforsaken town and dig up our money box. While I'm there, I'm gonna pay my respects to a few people."

"Is that a smart thing to do, Sammy?" Albert questioned. "Why not just put this all behind you and start fresh in another town?"

"I don't intend to spend more than a week or so in that town, but I think I need to have some fun at their expense." He looked pleased with his decision.

"Aren't you afraid they'll recognize you?" asked Clarence.

"You didn't, did you? They won't either," Sammy said as the line started to move.

The guard was hurrying them along. Albert was frantic. After he got out of this hellhole, he had no intention of sticking with Sammy, but to get away from him, he needed the money that was in the box.

Before disappearing through the door, Albert yelled back at Sammy, "Remember our oath!"

Clarence called over his shoulder, "Don't spend our money!"

The door closed behind them with a solid thunk.

Chapter 38

MOLLY WOKE UP.   Where was she? Slowly, she raised her
head and surveyed her surroundings. She sometimes wondered if
normal people ever got tired of waking up each morning in the
same place...their beds. But a computer chair? When she raised
her head from the desk, she bumped the computer and the black
screen came to life. She read the last sentence she had typed;
Bananas are twelve. Bananas are twelve?

Scratching her head, she tried to remember what would have
prompted her to type a sentence like that and, in the process, she
felt something unfamiliar on her forehead. Her mirror told the
story: there were ridges from sleeping on the desk's sharp edge.
Slowly, she stretched, made her way to the bed, and crawled in.

Yesterday's open house was an agent's bad dream come true.
Anyone with a lick of sense knew the danger they were placing
themselves in when they put an open sign on the lawn of a house.
It told the world, come get me! I'm alone!

Just thinking about the big-as-a-cannon gun Jerry/Dave
pointed at her made her heart pound and her mouth dry. Pulling
the pillow over her head, she relived those terrifying moments.
How had the bullet missed her? Either he was a terrible shot or
maybe he chickened out at the last second? Thankfully, the
builder took the news of his wrecked wall quite well. Telling him
that she may have sold his spec house before she told him about
the wall was a sneaky thing to do, but, she thought, timing is
everything.

Her head was still safely under the pillow when the thought of calling Dr. Parker at the sleep clinic propelled her out of bed and into the shower. While standing under the spray, her thoughts turned to breakfast and coffee. Then she remembered that the literature from the sleep clinic advised that coffee should be avoided. How could she start her day without coffee? She had many questions for the good doctor; she hoped he had some good answers.

DR. PARKER ANSWERED the phone.

"Hello, Molly! I was hoping you'd call."

"And I'm hoping you have an opening for me soon."

"Do I have an opening?" he groaned. "That's all I have, Molly. Are you sure you're up to it today? Once again, you made the morning paper!"

"I did? I didn't bother to read the paper this morning." She shuddered. "Reading a story about someone getting shot at is one thing, but the story takes on a personal note when you happen to be that someone." In a subdued voice she added, "I didn't want to read about the close call I had with death."

"I understand," he said quietly.

Molly asked, "So you can see me today?"

"What are you doing this morning? Better yet, what are you doing right now?"

Molly moaned. "Right now I am trying to convince myself that I can start the day without a cup of coffee."

Dr. Parker smiled. "Believe me, you'll live. There is a thing called decaffeinated coffee, you know."

"I wish I could say that makes me feel better, but it doesn't."

"How about dropping by at ten o'clock?" he asked. "Can you do that?"

"Thank you, Dr. Parker, I'll be there. Just the thought that you might have the answer to my crazy legs problem makes me giddy!"

She made a hurried call to instruct Clara to open the office at nine o'clock. She was hoping that her weekend ads would generate some interested calls.

THE SLEEP CLINIC HAD few people in the waiting room when Molly walked in. Dr. Parker's office was sparsely furnished, but Molly could see into one of the rooms that, in addition to medical equipment, contained a bed.

Molly's hand flew to her mouth. "Dr. Parker, will I have to spend the night here to prove to you that my legs won't let me sleep?"

"Only if I find you have obstructive sleep apnea or if I think you might have narcolepsy."

"Oh my!" she exclaimed. "Is either of those a possibility?"

"That's what we'll find out. So let's get started. I'll ring for my nurse and she'll help you get ready for the examination."

After some questioning and testing which established that Molly was in excellent health despite a chronic lack of sleep, Dr. Parker was ready to discuss her sleep problem.

Molly sat on the edge of her seat, waiting to hear what he had to tell her. From the history of her nightly battles, he concluded that she had neither apnea nor narcolepsy. Tests had ruled out a vast number of things, including kidney problems, iron deficiency, diabetes, and depression.

He had heard versions of Molly's story many times, told by men and women who were more than merely puzzled about their strange night doings; they were scared.

"Molly, since I've found no physical concerns, let's concentrate on the problem you're having at night with your legs."

"So if you didn't find anything wrong in the tests, do you know why I have such a problem?"

"No, I don't. What you have has been referred to as 'the most common disease you have never heard of: Restless Legs Syndrome'."

"Couldn't they have come up with a more sophisticated name for the syndrome?" Molly asked, wrinkling her nose. "Restless Legs sounds neither dignified nor serious."

"I can't say that I don't agree with you, Molly. It does have another name: Ekbom Syndrome. That name may sound more medical and less frivolous but you have to admit *Restless Legs* describes your legs at night, doesn't it?"

You're right," she admitted. With a big grin on her face she added, "You would be shocked at the names I've called it in the middle of the night. Believe me, my names are much more colorful and descriptive!"

"I have no doubt, Molly," he chuckled, "but you don't have to share them with me. I'll take your word for it."

Molly turned serious. "I was surprised to find that one out of every ten people suffers to some degree with this condition, so why haven't any of my doctors known about it?"

"Recently there has been a lot of information about this condition so there's no excuse for their not knowing about it," he answered. "I do believe you told me the other night that you had shared this problem with them."

"I certainly have! I must admit I haven't mentioned it to the doctors since I relocated here to take over Dad's business. I didn't want people in my new town to find out that a crazy person was running his real estate office. But before I moved here, I told them all; my gynecologist, my dermatologist, and even my dentist. They all were sympathetic, patted me on the back, and said they were sorry I was having so much discomfort."

He'd heard this before as well. "Did they suggest anything?"

"Besides sample pills that never worked, they suggested that stress and depression were causing my problem. But the biggest blow was when I was given a referral to a psychiatrist."

He waited a moment, gathering his thoughts; she wasn't expecting to hear what he was about to say. "You know, I have been telling you that this is not all in your head." He watched her nod. "But it is."

Molly's head snapped up. "What?"

"Considerable evidence suggests that the condition is related to a dopamine dysfunction in the brain's circuits. Dopamine is needed to produce smooth muscle activity, and any disruption results in involuntary movements."

"But Dr. Parker! You told me my problem wasn't in my head, and now you're telling me that it is?" she jumped to her feet. "I don't understand."

Dr. Parker spoke softly. "You're feeling that I'm not leveling with you, aren't you? Sit down, and I'll try to explain." He eased his hip onto the corner of his desk. "You'll need to get on the Internet and Google 'Restless Legs Syndrome'. That will take you to the Foundation's site where you'll find the answers to many of your questions. The Foundation also has a newsletter that you will receive if you join, which I suggest you do. You'll have access to all the research that has been done, and the progress that is being made."

"Like what?" Molly was still reeling over Dr. Parker's words

"At the Foundation's request, people with the condition were asked to donate their brains to research after death. The researchers wanted to determine if the brain of a person suffering with restless legs was different from the brains of those who don't have the problem."

"And…?" asked Molly.

"Yes, there are differences. They found during autopsies that some patients with the problem have subnormal levels of iron in the brain."

"So you're telling me that by taking more iron I would get rid of my problem?"

He shook his head, "No, I checked your iron, and it's fine."

Molly stomped her foot. "But none of this makes any sense!"

"You were hoping I could tell you the reason you have restless legs; I can't do that. You could have inherited it. Do you have any relatives who complain about legs that won't stay still? If you do, you have a three to seven times greater chance of having it yourself."

"I might have a relative who has it but doesn't want to share the information with the rest of the family. No one wants to be thought crazy." Molly almost smiled. "But no, I have never heard anyone in the family complain about funny legs except me."

"They have isolated the gene that carries the condition, so they are making progress in understanding it."

"I've made progress, too. Even though you can't tell me why I have it, I know the problem with my legs is real, that it has a name, and there is medication…." Molly's eyes narrowed. "Please don't tell me you've changed your mind about that, too."

"No, Molly," he grinned, "I haven't changed my mind about that; there really is help for your problem. There are several brands of medication that I can prescribe for you, and they all work on the same principle. The pills act either by directly stimulating the dopamine receptor by pretending to be dopamine, or by making it more sensitive to the dopamine that the body already has."

"Will they cure it?"

"Nothing will cure the problem, Molly, but the ingredient in the medicine will make your life much more livable."

"Can I start the pills today?" she asked eagerly. "Just the thought of a whole night's sleep is exciting!"

He smiled at her enthusiasm. "Here's the plan: There are several medications to choose from, and if one doesn't work, we'll move on and try another. Everyone is different; what works for one person doesn't necessarily work for someone else. It's seldom a matter of finding one medication and getting all the relief you expect."

Molly looked concerned. "Are you telling me the medicine you're going to prescribe might not work?"

"These medications don't come with the label 'one size fits all'," he said. "In many cases, people end up with cocktails of multiple drugs, and drug holidays where they take breaks from the medications that have become ineffective after long-term use."

"My goodness!" she said. "That sounds complicated."

"We'll work this out together. And I promise we'll find what works best for you."

She thought for a moment. "I have so many questions to ask you, Dr. Parker."

"Such as?"

"Why is it that my legs do their crazy thing at night and not in the day?"

"Some people do have symptoms during the day, but mostly they occur at night. All living things have a twenty-four hour rhythm...a circadian pattern. Symptoms usually occur in the evening or at bedtime. Are your sensations gone in the morning?"

"Yes, they are," she answered. "Most mornings I could sleep a few more hours if I didn't have to get up and go to work."

"Working people don't have the option of going back to sleep. For lack of sleep, surgeons have had to retire and airline pilots have been given desk jobs. But just like you, most people make it through the day in a state of fatigue."

Molly shook her head. "I can't tell you how many times I have fallen asleep at my desk. My secretary accuses me of being a vampire."

"I guess the symptoms fit a vampire's description…minus the neck biting. Any more questions?"

"Let's talk about coffee. I have a hard time getting started in the morning without my caffeine."

"You're not alone," Dr. Parker nodded. "I need my coffee, too."

"So, what do I do?"

"It's a personal thing, since Restless Legs affects people differently. You'll just have to see what works for you."

With a humorless laugh, she said, "I would imagine people have come up with strange things to get through the night when dawn seems a long ways away. One night I even fantasized cutting off my legs."

"I'm glad you didn't decide to solve your problem with such drastic measures!" he said as they laughed together. "Well, I do have one patient who claims that caffeine helps him. He drinks one of those high-caffeine bottled drinks before he goes to bed. Another patient takes a bath in vinegar. There is a section in the Foundation's newsletter that's called 'Bedtime Stories'. People send in the most outrageous stories of things they have come up with to get them through the night. I think that section is the most read part of the newsletter. Reading those stories, you get to understand that what works for one person, doesn't necessarily work for anyone else. Do you understand what I'm telling you?"

"I'm beginning to."

"Consider this your individual journey. Maybe a cup of coffee in the morning would be fine for you. You'll need to experiment with time and amounts, noting which combination works for you." He pulled out his pad, wrote on it, and then handed her a prescription.

Molly waved it in the air. "What were the chances that I would sell a house to the person who would solve my crazy leg problem?" She stepped closer and gave him a hug. "I can't wait to get this prescription filled. Will the pills work right away?"

"I predict that you will be pleasantly surprised tomorrow morning when you wake up in bed, rested, and ready for a new day."

A smiling Molly, prescription in her purse, drove off to find the nearest drugstore.

Chapter 39

SHOPPING BAG IN HAND, Molly arrived at the office just in time to find Clara ending a phone call.

"Molly!" she shrieked as the chair she so rapidly vacated crashed to the floor. Molly watched in dread as Clara rounded the desk and headed her way.

In defense, Molly bent her body and waited for the blow. Clara threw herself into Molly's arms with the force of a linebacker. Together they crashed into the wall and slid, still hugging, to the floor.

"Molly!" cried Clara. "You don't know how glad I am to see you!"

Molly was trying to push Clara away. "If you were any gladder, you probably would have killed me! Now will you get off me? Anyhow, we talked yesterday after the open house and you weren't this hysterical then, so why the big greeting now?"

"Ha, that's because yesterday I hadn't read this morning's paper, that's why! Wait until you read it yourself. The stuff they've found out about Jerry Miller! He's one scary dude!"

Molly reached out a hand and hauled Clara to her feet. "Thanks for the warning, Clara. I already have nightmares about what I do know. I don't need any more fuel to feed the fire for bigger and better ones!"

Clara picked up the package that Molly had dropped. Handing it to her, Clara asked hopefully, "Dare I hope there's something good to eat in there?"

"No, nothing to eat, but something even better."

"Not possible."

"Yes, possible. I saw Dr. Parker this morning, and he confirmed what my crazy legs do at night is called 'Restless Legs Syndrome'. What's in this package just might be the answer to my problem."

Clara looked skeptical. "You have magic pills in that package?"

"I sure hope so!"

MOLLY WATCHED CLARA gathering her things in preparation for closing the office. It was five o'clock Friday afternoon; both of them were more than ready to see the end of a very busy week.

"Whew," said Clara. I'm kinda sorry I was complaining about not having enough work to keep me busy. Boss, you sure outdid yourself this week."

"You never know in this business. Seems like it's either feast or famine. Sometimes I love this job, Clara," she confessed. "It's like playing Monopoly with someone else's money!"

Clara laughed. "Have any plans for the weekend?"

"Glad you mentioned it. How would you like to come to my house for a cookout on Sunday?"

"What?" Clara lifted an eyebrow. "No open house this Sunday?"

"I'm thinking of laying off for a few weeks," Molly shivered. "I get goose bumps just thinking about putting out open signs with an arrow pointing to where I will be."

Her thoughts went back to that horrible moment when Dave had touched her face and remnants of long-ago love made her knees go weak. How had her body betrayed her like that? She winced in disgust. Dave had called her 'an old maid school teacher'. It surprised her that he had even remembered that she had been a teacher. Maybe that was her destiny. An old maid was an old maid, and it didn't matter if she was a real estate agent or a school teacher. Either way, it was all the same.

Clara's voice brought her back to the present.

"Can't say that I blame you; that was scary business. But back to Sunday: would you believe my daughter Jill is leaving me with the two kids on Sunday so she can go to a party? Have you ever heard of such a thing as a purse party?"

"I have no comment about the purse party, but if you have the kids, just bring them with you. Mom and Tom have been hinting for an invitation to my house, so I've invited them, too."

"Well, if it's all right with you, sure. Can I bring anything else?"

Molly shook her head. "I'm just doing burgers and ribs on the grill, green salad, some potato salad… just cookout kind of stuff. Nothing fancy, so come around one o'clock.

GOD BLESS DR. PARKER! Nights were no longer something to be dreaded, and her bed was no longer her enemy. Even though Dr. Parker warned her that the medication wasn't 'one size fits all', so far the pills were working. There were no adverse side effects and no hangover feeling in the morning. She found that she could actually have coffee in the morning, but some other things, like chocolate late in the day, seemed to bother her. All was not perfect, but it certainly was an improvement.

SUNDAY MORNING MOLLY woke with a jerk. A quick look at the clock told her she had slept through the night and most of the morning. The magic pills had worked again, but almost too well. It was close to noon, and her guests were scheduled to arrive at one o'clock. If the pills worked this well, she was going to have to remember to set the alarm.

Mitch had been home a whole week, and while she had hoped and prayed, her phone never rang. How had everything gone so wrong?

He had to know about her brush with death. It would have been talked about at the station, and the papers were still full of the story. Even if he were just a friend, he could have called. Other friends had called, but he hadn't.

Pushing thoughts of Mitch out of her head, she pulled on an old pair of sweats, dragged her hair through a rubber band to make a ponytail, and slipped a pair of thongs on her feet.

A glance in the mirror made her smile because her eyes no longer had dark circles under them. God bless Dr. Parker!

Her smile faded as she skidded into the kitchen. There on the counter were the potatoes she had planned on making into potato salad this morning. How long did it take to peel, boil, and then turn the potatoes into something that resembled food? More time than she had, that was for sure!

Grabbing her car keys and purse, she headed for the deli. Along with the potato salad, she should buy some hot dogs for Clara's two grandkids, hot dog buns, pop, and a bag of charcoal. She had forgotten to buy charcoal! She hit herself on the forehead with the palm of her hand. How did this little cookout get so out of control?

By the time she returned home, her mother and Tom were sitting on the front porch steps.

Tom looked at his sister climbing out of the car and laughed. "You really didn't have to dress up for us, Mol. After all, we're just family."

"Stifle yourself, little brother. I woke up late and I'm way behind schedule."

"Here, let me help you," Tom said as he moved to take the bag of charcoal from her. The bag slipped out of his hands and split open when it hit the ground.

"Oh for heaven's sake! What a mess!" Molly wailed. "I don't have time for this! Mom, help Tom into the house with the rest of the bags and I'll clean this up."

Grabbing another container, she knelt and proceeded gingerly to pick up the sooty black briquettes. The sweat running down her cheeks was annoying, her knees hurt, and she was having thoughts that maybe a cookout wasn't such a good idea after all. She wiped the sweat off her forehead, picked up the bag, and headed into the house.

By the time she got back to the kitchen, her mother and Tom had things organized. The potato salad was in a charming little ceramic bowl and Molly had every intention of pretending that she had made it; Clara would be impressed.

"Mom, go out and sit at the picnic table," Molly ordered. "Tom can cook, and I'll set the table. When Clara comes, she can make the salad."

By the time Clara and the girls arrived, Tom had the fire going and the wonderful aroma of summer barbeque filled the air.

Molly smiled. Everything was turning out just fine even though she had overslept.

ON THE OTHER SIDE OF TOWN, Mitch and the girls were having a quiet Sunday. He put down the paper and watched the girls play a card game. His thoughts went to Molly once again, as they had been doing all week.

When he ran into Tom on Monday and learned that some terrible thing had happened at Molly's open house, he pretended to be uninterested.

Uninterested? The intensity of his feelings had shocked and surprised him. But why should he be so surprised? It had started the moment their eyes first met. A picture was engraved in his memory of the redheaded green-eyed woman, smiling at him with her hand held out in greeting. It didn't even matter that the greeting wasn't for him; Molly thought he was the buyer from Grand Rapids.

The more time he spent with her, the more his feelings for her deepened but Molly obviously didn't feel the same. Seeing her in the sandwich shop with another man confirmed this.

Even knowing that something bad had happened at her open house, he wasn't prepared for the horror of the actual details. The thought that she had nearly died brought him to tears.

Lying awake at night, he dreamed of hearing her voice. He tried to think of a reason to call her, but she had made it perfectly clear that she wanted nothing more to do with him.

Eventually his thoughts went back to the conversation with her brother. Tom claimed she was asleep. How could that be? The three of them had made enough noise to raise the dead. Although, he pondered, Tom did say that she walked at night because she had trouble sleeping, and she *was* out walking the night of the murders. Tom also said Molly felt so bad about the whole mix-up that she cried.

Then yesterday there was that phone call from Tom. While it wasn't exactly an invitation, he had mentioned a family gathering at Molly's on Sunday. Mitch made a quick decision. Doing nothing was getting him nowhere and, if she slammed the door in his face, at least he could tell himself that he'd tried.

"Girls, let's go for a ride!"

"Ice cream, Uncle Mitch, ice cream?" Kim's bright and hopeful face looked up at him.

"Maybe later. Right now I have a favorite tie that I need to get back from a very pretty lady."

A DISHEVELED MOLLY looked out the kitchen window, pleased at the success of her cookout. She picked up one of the pies that Clara had brought and headed for the backyard.

Emma and Hannah were playing by Molly's flower garden. Intrigued with the watering hose Molly had left after she had watered her plants yesterday, Hannah picked it up. Fumbling with the unfamiliar mechanism, she accidentally squirted Emma. Yelling in indignation, Emma chased her sister through Molly's flowers garden. It was payback time!

In all the commotion, no one had heard the arrival of Mitch and the girls.

"No sense in ringing the doorbell," commented Laurie. "We know it doesn't work."

Kim peered through the window and caught a glimpse of Molly in the kitchen holding something.

"I think I see a pie!" Kim clapped her hands. "Sometimes pie can be just as good as ice cream!"

"Looks like something is going on in the backyard," said Mitch. "Let's walk around the house quietly; if it's really a private party, we can leave."

"But if we leave, what about your favorite tie? You said we were here to get back your tie," Laurie reminded him.

"If I can't get it this time maybe I'll get it some other time." There was apprehension in Mitch's voice. Now that he had made up his mind to seek out Molly and hear her side of the story, he was feeling anxious that maybe it wasn't going to happen today. It surprised him just how much he wanted it all to work out.

The three of them rounded the corner of the house and stopped.

Tom, his back turned, was inspecting the smoky meat cooking on the grill. There was a picnic table that had place settings for six. On the table was a big pitcher of iced tea, a bowl of potato salad, and all the fixings for hot dogs, hamburgers, and ribs. He figured the woman who was seated at the table was Molly's mother, and beside her was the woman he recognized as Molly's secretary. He had no idea who the two young girls were.

The back door opened and Molly walked out, her arm raised with a pie balanced on her fingertips.

There she was. But wait! Was this the same woman he had been dreaming about? The woman he couldn't get out of his thoughts?

The Molly he was looking at didn't look like the Molly in his memory. This Molly had a head of red hair that hadn't seen a brush today; her baggy sweats were stained and her feet were bare. This Molly was even more beautiful than the one he remembered.

He started to lead his little group forward when Molly yelled, "Let's have a drum roll, please!"

Tom and Mom rapidly hit the palms of their hands on their thighs to produce the requested sound. Clara, not part of the Allen culture, looked on in amusement.

231

"Ladies and gentlemen!" Molly shouted like a carnival hawker. "May I present to you today's prize-winning pie, baked by my one and only secretary!"

"Oh, go on now," Clara protested. "I bought that pie at the same deli where you bought that potato salad. Right?"

While Tom's attention was away from the grill, the greasy spare ribs caught fire and flames blazed high.

An alarmed Emma grabbed the hose from Hannah, squeezed the handle, and sent a jet of water toward the fire. The fire sputtered out, leaving a sodden mess of meat on the grill. Hannah pushed Emma, reclaimed the hose, and sent out another jet of water. This one hit Molly squarely on the back of the head.

The pie shot out of her hands, landed upside down on the table by the pitcher of iced tea, which turned over and emptied itself into the bowl of potato salad.

The silence was deafening.

Then, from the side of the house, a man holding the hands of two little girls asked,

"Anyone for Happy Burgers?"

Chapter 40

A DRENCHED MOLLY came to an abrupt stop. She had heard
that question once before on the night when Mitch stood on her
porch holding the hands of two little girls. That was the night
when her cursed emerald green dress had once again dashed her
dreams, and the night that had opened her heart to dream once
more. Slowly, she turned around.

There, again, stood Mitch holding his nieces' hands.

"What are you doing here?" she blurted, her heart pounding.

Kim pulled her hand away from Mitch and ran toward her.
"He wants his tie back!" she said as she skidded to a stop.

"You came back for your tie?" Molly looked disbelievingly at
Mitch.

"I'm sure glad I didn't come for lunch," he said with a straight
face.

Molly, her dripping hair hanging around her charcoal-smeared
face, green eyes wide in disbelief, stared at Mitch. This had to be
a dream.

Tom extended his hand and walked toward him. "Glad you
could make it, Mitch. Don't think you'll get much to eat, though."

"You invited him?" Molly's voice quivered. "You know
Mitch?"

Tom pulled Mitch toward the group. "Mol, I was Mitch's
undercover plant in the gang."

Peggy jumped up. "Tom, you promised me you wouldn't do
anything I had to worry about!"

His face red, Tom hugged his mom and whispered, "Please quit acting like a mother!"

Peggy cuffed Tom on the back of his head.

"Oh, by the way, Mitch," Tom chuckled as he rubbed his head, "this lovely lady is our mother, Peggy Allen."

Molly watched as Mitch and her mother shook hands. So this wasn't a dream. She turned a puzzled face toward her brother.

"But the day we had lunch at mom's house I told you about Mitch, and you never said you knew him. Why didn't you tell me?"

"You never told me Mitch's last name," Tom answered.

"That explains it," Mitch said. "Tom knew me only as Detective Hatch. I'm glad we got that straightened out."

He turned to Molly. "Now, what about my tie?"

She smiled up at him, her green eyes sparkling, her dimples undiminished by the smears of charcoal dust. "Did you really come back just for your tie?"

I was right, thought Mitch. She does have two dimples. "Well, it is my favorite tie, but, no, Molly, that's not the reason I came today."

"A reason besides Tom's invitation?" Molly was thinking about her calls to Mitch.

Mitch looked at Molly and smiled. "Tom convinced me you had a good explanation for the night you didn't answer the door. I wanted to believe him so badly that I agreed to come and eat his cooking." Mitch paused, looked over the mess on the table, and grinned, "But it looks like I'll be spared that pleasure. Doesn't look like there's much left to eat."

Clara had been quiet during the whole debacle. She had never before seen a perfectly good cookout reduced to rubble in such a short time. "Wait a minute!" she cried. "There is food left. I brought two pies; the other one is still in the kitchen. By the way,

I think it's about time you introduced us to those beautiful little girls of yours. I know my grandkids would love to meet them."

Hannah and Emma, who had been hiding behind Molly's flowers, were wondering how long it was going to take before the grownups realized they were the ones who had ruined everything. Not knowing what the punishment would be was worse than any punishment could be, so they left their hiding place behind the tulips and walked slowly into the group.

To their surprise, no one yelled at them. Even Grandma Clara was smiling.

Mitch pulled his girls close. "These are my nieces, Kim and Laurie. And Clara, if the two who successfully demolished a fine cookout belong to you, I'm sure my girls would love to get to know them, too."

"Come here," Clara pulled her granddaughters to her side and scolded them. "Never thought you would be such a problem or I wouldn't have brought you in the first place!"

"Go easy on them, Clara," Peggy urged. "Someday we'll look back on this day and have a good laugh."

"How many years do you figure that might take?" Clara snorted. "Anyhow, this one is Emma; she's the one who put out the grill fire. That leaves Hannah here as the one who squirted Molly on the back of the head." Clara ended the sentence snickering.

Tom took the laughter up a notch with a loud guffaw. Peggy let loose with a hoot and doubled over with laughter. Molly and Mitch joined the merriment, and soon the back yard rang with happy sounds.

When the laughter died down and wet eyes were dried, Mitch, his heart in his eyes, looked at Molly. "Did you know I was out of town when all those bad things happened to you?" he asked softly.

Molly looked down, and then raised her eyes to his. "Your answering machine told me that."

"Molly," he stopped to take a deep breath, "if something really bad had happened and I never had the chance to see you again...." His voice caught as he asked, "Do you think we could start over?"

"You mean the cookout? Not really. I've no more hot dogs."

Relieved, Mitch grinned as he tucked a dripping hunk of hair behind her ear, pulled her close and said, "Frankly, my dear, I don't give a damn!"

Tom, who was listening while throwing soggy meat into a garbage bag, called out, "I heard that!" With a snicker he added, "I hate to tell you this, buddy, but that line's been used before!"

Peggy and Clara moved closer to the couple.

Mitch pulled Molly further away and turned his back to them. "No, silly," he said quietly. "I'm not talking about the cookout. I'm talking about us."

"Us?" she was almost afraid to ask, "Is there an 'us', Mitch?"

A flood of unwanted memories shut down her senses. Dave had used the same words: "What about us?" She shook off the thought.

Mitch, surprised at the intensity of his feelings, answered softly, "I'd dearly love to think so, Molly."

"But I don't understand. When you didn't answer my phone calls, I just figured..."

"Your phone calls?" He leaned back, looking surprised.

"Are you going to pretend you didn't get my calls?" she asked, her voice sharp.

"You called my cell phone?"

Molly nodded.

He visibly relaxed. "Please believe me when I tell you that I lost my cell phone! I haven't seen it since, ah" he stopped to think.

"The night when I didn't answer the door?"

"That's right," he nodded. "I have no idea where it is. Did you leave me messages?"

"Yes I did. When you didn't return my calls," Molly choked back a sob.

"Oh, Molly!" He buried his face in her soggy hair. "I'm sorry! I didn't know about those messages!" He dabbed at a tear running down her cheek.

He relished the feeling of finally having her in his arms. Fortunately, his good sense told him this was not the time to ask about her lunch companion.

"But what about all the bad things that happened?" she sputtered. "Don't you want to know why I didn't answer the door that night?"

"Tom clued me in. Anyhow," his eyes twinkled, "you'll have a lot of time to tell me all about it."

"A lot of time? I don't understand."

"Sure you do, Molly." His heart was beating so loud he was sure she could hear it. "I can see it in your eyes."

Molly blushed. "Is it that obvious?"

"Yes," he said with a catch in his voice, "and my heart would be broken if I didn't see it there."

The small group edged closer to the pair. They cheered when he wiped the grime off her face and kissed her.

Mitch could feel his broken heart healing as he hugged Molly and cried, "We need to celebrate!"

"Happy Burgers?" suggested Laurie.

Mitch looked down at Molly's beaming face. His heart was so full of love that he swung her around and kissed her again.

"Forget Happy Burgers," he cried. "This calls for champagne!"

THE COOKOUT WAS OVER, the kitchen cleaned, Tom had taken Kim and Laurie to Mitch's parents, and the rest of the guests were gone. Well, not all of them.

The one remaining guest, Mitch, was slouched on the couch, his feet on the coffee table, and a beer in his hand. "Beer beats champagne every time," he grinned.

Molly, her hair still wet from a much-needed shower, managed a nod of agreement and a toast with her own bottle. How could a day that had started out so hectic end so wonderfully? She sat down beside Mitch and when his arms gathered her to him, she thought her heart would burst.

Mitch nuzzled her ear. "Have you changed your mind about commitments now?" he asked.

"About what?" she murmured.

"Remember when you told me, and I'm quoting you here, 'I'll take a routine uneventful life over a tumultuous one any old day'?"

Molly was quiet for a bit. "I can't believe you remembered my exact words!"

"You didn't answer my question."

She thought for a moment. Then, holding his face between her hands, she kissed him softly on the lips.

"Humm. That felt like a yes."

Overcome by emotion, she just nodded.

All was silent for a few moments as they gazed into each other's eyes. Molly, her hands still holding his face, was about to kiss him again, when an idea popped into her head. Her face lit up, her eyes twinkled, and her dimples deepened.

It was a *brilliant* story idea!

There would be no writer's block when she wrote her next story. She knew the events, she knew the characters, and she knew the plot.

The ending, with her right here in Mitch's arms, would not really be an ending.

It would be the beginning of another story.

EPILOGUE

SAMMY THE GRUNT held his body rigid and his eyes expressionless. He kept that pose until his bus passed, unchallenged, through the gate and sped away from the Federal prison. With a satisfied grin, he allowed himself the luxury of looking back at the receding sight of the prison. He was a free man.

The release had taken much more time than Sammy figured it would; the wheels of justice truly did grind slowly. All morning long, he had been apprehensive, expecting at any moment a retraction of his release.

There had been no retraction.

At Sammy's insistence, the lawyer had arranged for his release before his two accomplices, Clarence and Albert. They remained housed in the prison that was rapidly fading away behind him.

Sammy grinned to himself, recalling the money and stolen identities in the hidden box the three of them had sworn to share equally. By the time Clarence and Albert got out, the box would be empty and he would be long gone and far away.

Happy with his own thoughts, he relaxed for the first time in days, leaned back in his seat and let the bus take him back to the small town in northern Michigan that a cellmate had once called 'God's country'.

About the Author

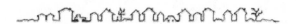

EVELYN WOULD LOVE to hear from you. If you have comments about *And So To Sleep*, the first book in the Accidental Mystery Series, you can contact her at evharp@hotmail.com, or you can find out more about her on her website:
http://www.evelynallenharper.com/

Evelyn lives with her husband, Barry, in a home they built on the shores of lovely Pearl Lake near Empire, Michigan. She loves pets and currently shares her home with a rescued dog named Earl, and with a semi-tame feral cat named Simon.

The daughter of a coal miner, Evelyn left the hills of Pennsylvania to attend Anderson College in Indiana and then to Michigan where she earned a Masters at Wayne State University.

She taught school until the birth of her two children, Jill and Tom. A constant delight in her life is her stepdaughter, Judith.

A Realtor for many years, some of Molly's real estate adventures happened to Evelyn, but most are fiction.

She has suffered with Restless Legs Syndrome all her adult life.

PROLOGUE

AND SO TO DREAM

LOST, SAMMY THE GRUNT CURSED the back roads as he pulled his car to a stop near a well-lit barn. Someone in there had to know how to get back to that little hick town, back to his buried treasure, and back to settle the score with those who had sent him to prison.

Upon entering the barn, Sammy quickly realized he had stumbled into pleasantly familiar surroundings, a dogfight. The raucous crowd quieted as a man with a beard and stomach that would put Santa to shame, announced the next two fighters. Because the dog matched the color of his name, Sammy knew right away which one was 'Old Yellow', but why would that hefty, male dog be called 'Girly'?

Sammy loved the viciousness of a good dogfight. With a dazzling white smile, he pushed his way to the center of the action, and placed his bet.

Booing and shouts of anger filled the barn as Girly ambled over to the challenger, and sat down. Old Yellow circled the big black dog, snarling a few times before he too, sat down.

Disgusted with the lack of action, Sammy grabbed a long stick with a pointed end and poked the black dog. He repeatedly jabbed Girly while several men sent him disapproving looks.

Sammy's vicious thrusts continued until the bloodied dog turned his head to look directly into Sammy's eyes.

The intensity of Girly's look sent a chill down Sammy's spine. He dropped the stick.

When he noticed a scowling man pushing his way through the crowd towards him, Sammy scooted out the door and began running towards his car just as the black dog rushed past him and disappeared into the dark woods.

The last thing Sammy heard from the barn was the Santa-like man screaming, "Girly, you worthless bucket of chicken-shit, git back here!"

Safe in his car, Sammy escaped through the black night, none the wiser as to where he was, and none the wiser as to the unknowing innocents this winding road would lead him to.

9 781609 106225